MEMORIES OF THE BEACH

KAY CORRELL

ZURA LU PUBLISHING, LLC

This book is dedicated to the many hours I've spent at the beach. The sunshine, the birds soaring overhead, the sound of the waves hitting the shore. Laughing with family and friends. I find peace and joy at the beach. I hope you will too in the pages of this book.

KAY'S BOOKS

Find more information on all my books at
kaycorrell.com

COMFORT CROSSING ~ THE SERIES
The Shop on Main - Book One
The Memory Box - Book Two
The Christmas Cottage - A Holiday Novella
(Book 2.5)
The Letter - Book Three
The Christmas Scarf - A Holiday Novella
(Book 3.5)
The Magnolia Cafe - Book Four
The Unexpected Wedding - Book Five

The Wedding in the Grove - (a crossover short

story between series - with Josephine and Paul from The Letter.)

LIGHTHOUSE POINT ~ THE SERIES
Wish Upon a Shell - Book One
Wedding on the Beach - Book Two
Love at the Lighthouse - Book Three
Cottage near the Point - Book Four
Return to the Island - Book Five
Bungalow by the Bay - Book Six

CHARMING INN ~ Return to Lighthouse Point
One Simple Wish - Book One
Two of a Kind - Book Two
Three Little Things - Book Three
Four Short Weeks - Book Four
Five Years or So - Book Five
Six Hours Away - Book Six
Charming Christmas - Book Seven

SWEET RIVER ~ THE SERIES
A Dream to Believe in - Book One
A Memory to Cherish - Book Two
A Song to Remember - Book Three
A Time to Forgive - Book Four

A Summer of Secrets - Book Five
A Moment in the Moonlight - Book Six

MOONBEAM BAY ~ THE SERIES
The Parker Women - Book One
The Parker Cafe - Book Two
A Heather Parker Original - Book Three
The Parker Family Secret - Book Four
Grace Parker's Peach Pie - Book Five
The Perks of Being a Parker - Book Six

BLUE HERON COTTAGES ~ THE SERIES
A six-book series coming in 2022.
Memories of the Beach - June 23, 20022

WIND CHIME BEACH ~ A stand-alone novel
- May 17, 2022

INDIGO BAY ~ A multi-author sweet romance series

Sweet Days by the Bay - Kay's Complete Collection of stories in the Indigo Bay series

Sign up for my newsletter at my website *kaycorrell.com* to make sure you don't miss any new releases or sales.

ABOUT THIS BOOK

Violet Bentley bought the run-down Blue Heron Cottages and updated the small beachside resort in the quaint town of Moonbeam. Her brother, Rob, is temporarily living with her in the owner's cottage and helping with the resort. She adores him—really she does—he's all the family she has. And if he'd just keep his many opinions to himself, it would be the perfect arrangement.

Aspen is stuck in a stream of bad luck and can't seem to break her streak. She receives a mysterious letter asking her to come to an all-expenses-paid week at the resort. She's intrigued but can't afford to take time off work. When her boss fires her, the decision is made. She packs up all her belongings and heads for Moonbeam, curious about the letter and nowhere else to go.

Still grieving the loss of her mother, Willow receives her own letter asking her to come to the resort. She's uncertain, but her husband encourages her to go. Maybe it has something to do with what her mother struggled to tell her—unsuccessfully—with her dying breaths. And Willow has to admit a week at the beach and time to relax might be just what she needs.

What neither woman sees coming are the startling revelations the letters will bring to their lives.

Memories of the Beach is the first book in a heartwarming series about Violet, the charming people of Moonbeam, and the guests who come to stay at Blue Heron Cottages.

CHAPTER 1

"You could always move out." Violet Bentley glared at her brother, Rob, after one too many of his *helpful* suggestions.

"I just think you need to find some more help. You can't keep running the resort all by yourself," Rob insisted. "I don't mind helping out. Really. But you need to find a more permanent solution."

"Sorry I've been such a bother."

"Come on, Vi, don't be like that. I enjoy helping. Even if I thought you were crazy for buying the cottages, it turned out to be a great idea. You've done a fantastic job. I predict Blue Heron Cottages will be a huge success. I'm proud of you, sis."

Now she felt rotten that she'd suggested he move out. "Thanks. And I didn't mean the moving out thing."

"But you're right. I can't just live here with you rent-free forever. It is time to look for my own place."

Now she'd messed it all up. She didn't really want him to move out of the owner's suite. She enjoyed his company, even if he was over-eager in the advice-giving department. And to be honest, she'd have never gotten the resort remodeled and opened without his help.

"But you can live here forever, Robby."

"Because you like my help." His mouth tilted into a grin. "But really, I've been thinking about getting a place down the beach. I'll still be near. Just not underfoot all the time. I can still help out when you need me."

"You probably need quiet. I have taken you away from your writing. I'm sorry." She tried to give him quiet time in the cottage each day for his writing, but it always seemed like something popped up. A leaky pipe, a stuck door, a loose porch plank. And Rob was one of the handiest people she knew. He always jumped up to fix it for her. Though she'd been pretty proud of herself when she fixed that stuck window in the teal cottage. Even put some goo-stuff on it so it hopefully wouldn't get stuck again.

If Rob moved out, she really needed to find a handyman who could fix the things she couldn't fix herself. Or maybe she'd just YouTube herself into becoming an accomplished handywoman. That might work.

"I've actually gotten a lot of writing done since I've moved to Moonbeam. More than usual, once I got past my writer's block. But I think it's time to find my own place."

"I love having you here, but if you need your own space, I get it. I'm not always the easiest person to live with."

He threw his head back, and laughter rolled across the room. "No, you're not the easiest."

"You don't have to say it like that." She stepped back and glared at him once again.

"Sis, you are the messiest, most opinionated, constantly moving person I've ever lived with."

"I might leave a *few* things lying around." She glanced around the main room of the owner's suite at the dirty dishes on the counter, two opened boxes of supplies sitting by the door, a sun hat resting precariously on the back of a chair, and the book she'd been reading spread open on the sofa. Oh, and two pairs of shoes in various spots on the floor. But she'd pick all those up real soon now, ignoring the fact they had all been there for days. "But for the record, you're not the best roommate I've ever had either." Though, he really was…

"So, really. You're going to be okay with me moving out?"

"Of course," she lied. "It's fine." He probably wanted some privacy now that he was dating Evelyn. She couldn't fault him for wanting a space to be alone with her.

"So you'll get someone to help you here?" he reiterated.

"I can handle it all on my own," she insisted while snatching the hat off the back of a chair and putting it on a hook by the door where it belonged. She nonchalantly walked over to the sink and picked up a glass, rinsed it, and put it in the dishwasher.

"I still think you need help," Rob said yet one more time before turning back to his laptop and pecking away at the keys.

He was probably right, but she would never admit that to him. It would only encourage more *ever-so-helpful* suggestions.

She'd figure something out. It wasn't like the resort was bringing in tons of revenue yet. She was still paying off some of the repairs and remodeling, with a list of ones still to do.

The bell rang at the front desk in the reception area attached to the owners' cottage. "Gotta get that," she said as she walked to the connecting door.

"If you had someone helping you, they could get it," Rob muttered.

"I heard that," she tossed back over her shoulder.

She entered the reception area to greet an older woman standing by the desk. Her gray hair was cut in a bob, just grazing her shoulders. She gave Violet a smile that didn't quite reach her eyes. A sadness lurked there.

"Good afternoon. May I help you?"

"I have a reservation. Or I did. I'm not sure now. You see, I come here every year the first week of September. But it was Murphy's Resort. Now I see it's Blue Heron Cottages."

"I'm sorry. When Murphy sold me the place, he didn't tell me about any standing reservations. And I did rename the place. But I do have some vacancies." This lady was actually only her third rental for the week. A vacancy rate she wasn't pleased with.

"You wouldn't happen to have the last one, would you? The little one-bedroom at the end?"

"I sure do. It's been updated and remodeled."

"Oh." The lady didn't look very happy about that.

"It has air-conditioning now. A new mattress. And it's painted a pretty peach color. Oh, and the kitchen sink doesn't drip anymore." She laughed. "But otherwise, it's pretty much the same." Well, and the roof didn't leak anymore either…

"Could I have it for the week?"

"Sure can. Let's get you registered. Just one guest?"

"Yes, just me," the woman said quietly. "Rose Sherman."

"Well, Mrs. Sherman, we'll get you signed in and I'll give you the key."

"Oh, call me Rose, please."

"Rose it is." She handed the key to her. "Do you need any help with your bags?"

"No, I'll be fine. Thank you." The woman gave another smile that didn't quite break through the sadness in her eyes, then turned and walked out of the door.

So Rose Sherman used to come to Murphy's Place every year. Hmm, wonder what the story was on that.

CHAPTER 2

Aspen Caldwell frowned at the letter from Brown and Bates Law Firm. What now? It's never good news from lawyers, is it? She was tempted to throw it in the trash, but she slowly slit the envelope open and held her breath as she read the letter on the firm's letterhead. The letter told her to see the enclosed note.

She fished in the large envelope and pulled out a wrinkled piece of cream paper, different than the crisp, white, heavy-weight letterhead.

She gasped when she recognized the handwriting, even after all these years. Her mother's.

Aspen,

If you're reading this, it means my lawyer found you, and I certainly hope he did. I know I disappeared from your life. Then when I went to find you, I couldn't. You'd moved.

No kidding, she'd moved. Her mother had packed up and left her alone in their apartment three months before her high school graduation. Her mom had bragged about how her boyfriend of the month paid the rent until the end of May for her. Only after her mom left, she found out he really hadn't. So Aspen took on a second job as she struggled to finish school for those three months. All alone. And while other kids had family cheering them on at graduation, it had been completely quiet when she walked across the stage to get her diploma.

She thought she'd forgotten the hurt. After all, it had been more than twenty years, and she'd resolutely pushed all memory of it from her mind. But the pain still dug at the far corner of her heart.

She turned back to the letter.

. . .

I've arranged for you to go to Murphy's Resort the first week of September. It's all paid for. Please go. I have a bit of a surprise for you. A truth about your past.

I made rather a mess about being a mother. You deserved better.

And please, please go to Murphy's. I promise it will be worth it.

Magnolia

Not love, Mom. Not love, Magnolia. Just Magnolia. Which was fine, because she was certain her mother hadn't loved her. But she'd made peace with that. Okay, pretty much so. That far corner of her heart tweaked again.

And she noticed her mother didn't say she was sorry, just admitted to being a mess of a mother. So was her mother going to show up at this Murphy place? Show up after all this time?

A part of her didn't want to give her mother the satisfaction of doing what she'd requested. She didn't want to let her mother get the last word in. Because she didn't owe her mother anything. Nothing at all.

But curiosity was getting the best of her.

What was all this secrecy about? She read the lawyer's letter again, and all it said was that

Murphy's was now called Blue Heron Cottages, a reservation was made in her name for the first week of September, and to read the enclosed letter.

She chewed her lip. She would have to ask off work. Her waitress job didn't pay much, and tips were rotten in this out-of-the-way small town. But waitressing, working retail at a discount store, and cooking at a fast-food place were all she'd ever done.

A week off of work would make things tight. She could barely cover her rent and food. Luckily, she'd found a studio apartment right by the diner where she worked. So mostly the car just sat in its parking space except for a couple of trips a month to the discount supermarket out on the edge of town where groceries were cheaper. Maybe she'd eat mac and cheese for a bit and skip some meals. Wasn't intermittent fasting a thing now? She could call it that. Sounded much better than not being able to afford much food.

And surely her boss would give her the week off. Probably. Now if her old car would just get all the way to this town of Moonbeam and back. Plus gas money. Ugh. How would she make this work?

But she had to admit her mother had piqued her interest. What truth about her past? She knew everything about her childhood, and from the few memories she allowed herself to recall, it had been lousy. Her mother would disappear for days at a time, even when Aspen was only in grade school. She'd always been deathly afraid someone would find out and come take her away.

They moved at least twice a year. Often running out on the last few months of rent and leaving in the middle of the night. Her education suffered since she was always scrambling to adjust to a new school. She'd been grateful when they actually stayed in one place her senior year of high school. Well, *she'd* stayed in one place. Her mother had left.

And then Aspen left the day after graduation, taking a bus far away. She got a job waitressing at a truck stop where the bus had stopped. Found a tiny apartment and started on a series of crummy jobs and even crummier apartments. A never-ending cycle.

She stared at the letter again, debating what to do. And what if the line about the cottage being paid for was similar to her mother's boyfriend paying the rent for three months? Just another lie.

Finally, curiosity won. And she grudgingly admitted she'd like the chance to see her mother again, though she wasn't sure why.

With that decided, she promised herself that she'd ask off when she went in to work her shift tonight.

Willow Sampson stared at the letter from a legal firm in a place called Moonbeam. The letter was way too vague as far as she was concerned. But when she called for more information, the lawyer said he had to respect his client's wishes, and that all she was to know at this time was to go to this renamed Murphy's Resort the first week in September. There was a reservation in her name.

Then there was the handwritten letter.

Willow,

I'm hoping this letter finds its way to you. There are things you need to know. I've made a reservation for you at Murphy's Resort for the first week of September. It's all paid for. There are things I think you should know about your past. Or maybe you already know part of the truth. I'm not sure. But you should know the whole truth.

Please, please go to Murphy's. I promise it will be worth it.

M

She turned to her husband, Derek. "I don't think I'm going to go."

"Aren't you at least curious?" He wrapped his arms around her, pulling her close, and she sunk into his familiar embrace.

"A bit. But I don't see why I need to travel to Moonbeam to find out what this person is talking about. I don't even know if 'M' is a woman or a man."

"I think you should go. It will give you a break. And you know your mom was trying to tell you something when she died. Maybe it's this? Maybe this will explain things."

Willow closed her eyes, willing herself not to cry. It was still hard, ten months later, to think of her mom. She'd died so suddenly. Neither of them had been expecting it. Her mom got sick, and the doctors spoke of all these treatments to try... but within months, she was gone. And at the very end, her mother had struggled to tell her something in weak, faint words.

"I need... to... tell... Your past..." Her mother had gasped the words.

She'd leaned close to listen, but her mom had been too weak to say more.

Now this letter.

A letter promising that she would find out about her past.

"Let's all go," she said. Maybe they could make a quick vacation out of the trip.

"I can't. I'm hammered at work. And Eli will have just started back to school. Not a great time to pull him out."

"But what about Eli? Who will take care of him?"

"I'll get Mom to come over and watch him after school. It will be fine. You could use a break, anyway. You work, take care of Eli, take care of me. Volunteer at the school. You never take time for yourself. Wouldn't you love a week at the beach?" Derek encouraged her.

Though she'd expect no less from him. He was the most giving, caring, supportive person she'd ever met. She had to admit, a week away from the hubbub and chaos that was their life sounded nice. But then she immediately felt guilty.

But Eli would love spending time with his grandmother after school. He'd probably be spoiled rotten by the time she made it back home.

"I admit I'm curious. But I'd miss you two."

"It's a week, babe. You can sleep in, walk the beach, go shelling. You love to go shelling. We'll video chat each night before Eli goes to bed."

"You trying to get rid of me?" She punched him lightly in the arm.

"Not a chance." He kissed her gently on the lips, pulling her close.

"I guess I could drive down there. I think it's about four hours from here. Maybe I'll find out this mysterious news and be able to come right back home."

"Or you could just stay there and enjoy yourself."

She leaned her face against his chest, listening to his heartbeat. She wasn't sure how she'd gotten so lucky to find him, but she thanked her lucky stars every day that she had. They had the perfect marriage, with a wonderful son. Her own parents had been great role models for parenting, though her father died just as she graduated from college with her MBA. She'd found a job back home and moved in with her mother for a year to help her through the transition to being a widow. But her mom had encouraged her to get out on her own again.

Lucky for her, she'd found the perfect little townhouse… and Derek had lived next door. The rest, as they say, was history. A perfect life together.

She had to admit, her mom's last words had haunted her. Maybe it would be okay to just go to Moonbeam and see what was going on.

"You've decided you're going, aren't you?"

She looked up into Derek's eyes. "How did you know?"

"Just did." He pulled her close again.

CHAPTER 3

Things didn't work out exactly as Aspen had planned. So much for her boss giving her time off. He fired her instead, three days before she was scheduled to leave. She didn't have rent money for next month, so she let her apartment go. In truth, it wasn't much to let go of. And the job was lousy with a cranky boss and irregular work hours. She'd been thinking of moving on and finding something new, anyway. This just pushed her to do it sooner than she'd planned.

At least she had a place to stay for a week. A cottage in Moonbeam.

The miles rolled past as she drove down the highway, windows open, her hair flying in all directions. She turned up the radio and sang along to a sad ballad. Anything to chase her problems away. Singing about someone else's woes seemed a better choice.

She would have to find a job as soon as this whole mystery was over. And a new place to live, although she'd lived in her car before for a week here and there. She could certainly do it again if she had to. At least Florida was warm. She'd spent a week living in her car in a small town outside Denver one late autumn. Now that had been chilly.

She drove through Moonbeam and down its quaint streets. An actual general store, Parker's General Store, adorned one corner of the main street in town with a small cafe beside it. She'd have to pop in there to see it—not that she had any money to spend. She needed to hoard her meager savings. If three hundred and eighteen dollars to her name was considered savings. Cash. Carefully hidden in a carved-out book stashed in one of the boxes in her trunk.

She pulled up to Blue Heron Cottages, and a flitter of something ran through her. Like a bit of deja vu, which of course was silly. She'd never been to Moonbeam, much less this cute little cottage resort. But it reminded her of something… She just wasn't sure what. Pushing the strange feeling aside, she slipped out of the car and stretched after the long drive. The hot air surrounded her, and the sun rained down cheerful beams of light. Sure was hot and humid for September, though maybe southwest Florida was always like this in September. What did she know?

She looked around the resort, half expecting —half hoping?—to see her mother. But no.

She walked into the reception area— blissfully air-conditioned—and rang a bell on the counter. A woman hurried out from the back. "Hi, welcome to Blue Heron Cottages."

"Hi. I should have a reservation? Prepaid. Aspen Caldwell." It better darn well be prepaid because she sure couldn't afford a cottage right on the beach. And if this whole paid thing did end up being like when her mother lied about her boyfriend paying the rent on her apartment back in her high school days, she'd just turn around and leave. She probably didn't have enough money for even one night's stay here.

"I have the reservation right here. Yes, all paid for. For a week, right?"

"Right." A wave of relief swept through her.

"And I'm supposed to give you this

envelope." The woman handed it to her, and she stuffed it in her purse. Another envelope. And she recognized the formal return address now from Brown and Bates Law Firm.

"The mint green cottage. It's right across the courtyard and…" The woman smiled. "It's… well, mint green. Can't miss it. And I'm Violet, the owner. If you need anything, just ask."

"Thank you, I will. Do you happen to have a Magnolia…" She'd no idea what her mother's last name would be now. "Magnolia Caldwell staying here?"

"No, no one by that name."

"Okay, thanks." She took the key and headed out. She grabbed a suitcase from the backseat, ignoring the fact that all her earthly goods were in the trunk. She hadn't wanted it to look so obvious that she was living out of her car.

A thin, beautiful blonde woman was sitting on the porch of the yellow cottage next door. As she climbed the stairs to her cottage, the woman looked over and smiled at her. Chills ran through her as she lifted her hand in a small wave. Chills. That was strange. This place was making her jumpy, off-kilter. She was probably just tired from the long drive.

She opened the door and tugged her suitcase inside. She gasped in surprise. To her, the small cottage seemed like a luxury suite. Bright light flowed in through the many windows. A cheerfully painted table and chairs sat next to the small kitchenette. She kicked off her shoes and padded across the worn wooden floor. A bathroom with a white tile shower and two sinks. Two sinks! Then a bedroom with a king-sized bed and a tropical bedspread with monstera leaves printed on it.

She flopped down onto the bed and stretched her arms wide. This had to be the finest place she'd ever stayed. And it was all hers. At least for the week.

Remembering the letter from the law firm, she reluctantly climbed off the bed, went back to the front room, and fished the envelope out of her purse. She held her breath as she opened it, uncertain if she could stand another surprise or mystery.

She read the note and frowned. A meeting downtown tomorrow morning with the lawyer at ten. With a Sam Brown. Maybe all this mystery would be revealed then. She looked in the envelope and her mouth dropped open. A gift certificate to a Jimmy's on the Wharf.

Another one to a place called Brewster's. And two hundred dollars to Parker's General Store with a note to use it if she needed anything and that it could also be used at Sea Glass Cafe. Then three one-hundred-dollar bills for incidentals. She was suddenly a rich woman. Doubled her net worth in minutes. She clutched the bounty to her chest and felt like jumping for joy.

Always practical, she decided to stash the three hundred dollars. If Parker's General Store had any groceries or staple items, she'd buy things there and stow them in her trunk for food in the coming weeks.

With the thought of food, her stomach rumbled. She hadn't stopped to eat anything today because she was trying to conserve her cash.

A binder with local attractions sat on the table. She grabbed it and leafed through it. Ah, a menu from Jimmy's. She smiled in delight at the reasonable prices. She could get quite a few meals out of her gift certificate with some smart ordering. Brewster's was mainly a coffee place but had light breakfast fare and sandwiches. Looked like her meals for the week were covered.

A knock came at the door and she went to answer it. Violet stood there with a large basket. "Got this delivery for you from the market."

"I didn't order anything."

"It has your name on it."

"Really?" She reached for the overflowing basket.

"Yep, just came."

"Do you know who sent it?" She stared at the bounty.

"No. Just the regular delivery boy from the market. No note."

"Well, thank you."

"No problem. Enjoy." Violet headed back across the courtyard.

Aspen set the basket on the table and dug through it. Coffee, cream, quart of milk. A variety of teas. Bread. Butter. A jar of preserves. Snack mix. A few small boxes of cereal. Two apples, two bananas—which she hated—and a container of nuts. And look at that, a bottle of red wine and a bottle of white. Wow, she was set. So far this week was turning out better than she'd planned. Well, except for that whole getting fired thing.

A smile spread across her face and she twirled around, flinging her arms wide. Might as well enjoy every minute of this week. With that, she snatched up the gift certificate to Jimmy's. After searching for the restaurant on the map on her phone, she decided to walk there for her dinner. Not too far. Might as well save on gas. The unexpected gifts pouring in weren't going to last forever.

Aspen didn't really pay attention to the most direct route to the wharf and ended up wandering the town a bit, but she didn't mind. The sun was dipping lower, but she still kept to the shaded sidewalks. She finally ended up at the wharf and slowly strolled down it, looking at the shops lining both sides. Gift shops, a candy shop, women's fashion, a small art gallery. White Christmas lights were strung across the walkway, making the whole place look magical, like something out of a Christmas movie, even if it was just the first week in September.

When she reached Jimmy's, she was delighted to see the large outside eating area. The hostess sat her at a table near the edge with a wonderful view of the harbor and a nice breeze blowing to chase off the humidity. She'd never eaten at a place like this, right on the water. A man played the guitar on a small stage at the far end. Laughter rang out from the groups of people sitting around her. She glanced around to see if she was the only person eating alone.

Far across the seating area, one lone woman sat eating by herself. She frowned as a tingle ran through her. She was sure that was the same blonde woman she'd seen back at the cottages when she first arrived.

She turned back to the menu, ignoring the feeling of unease, and concentrated on the six-page menu. Six pages. The menu at the diner she'd just been fired from had all their choices on a single page. And lousy food. Everything here looked wonderful, but the choices overwhelmed her.

A man walked by with a Jimmy's on the Wharf t-shirt on. "Excuse me." She raised a hand to stop him. "Do you work here?"

"I, uh… yes. May I help you?"

"I was wondering what you'd suggest I order. Everything looks great."

He laughed. "That is one thing Jimmy's is known for. Lots of great food. You like seafood?"

"I do."

"Well, the grouper is great. Order a side of hushpuppies."

That did sound good. Though maybe she wouldn't get the side order so she wouldn't spend so much of the gift certificate on her first trip to Jimmy's.

"Though the onion rings are good, too. And the coleslaw. And our fries…" The man laughed again. "Anyway, you get a choice of two sides with the grouper."

Better yet. "Okay, thanks for your suggestions."

The man raised his hand and flagged a server. "Billy, will you take this lady's order? Pretty sure she's going to order the grouper. And give her a drink on the house."

"Sure thing, Mr. Bodine."

The man—Mr. Bodine—gave her a friendly smile and walked away, disappearing inside.

"Mr. Bodine?" She looked at Billy.

"Yep, the owner. Well, the owner's son. Jimmy Bodine, his father, owns the restaurant, but rumor has it that Walker—that was Walker Bodine—is going to take over soon."

"Oh." She'd thought he was just some server. Floating through life like she was.

Jumping from waitress job to waitress job to random other jobs. But no. He looked to be about her age and he was going to run the whole restaurant. But then, he'd been born into the job, she consoled herself. A family business. She hadn't had quite the successful family upbringing.

"So, you want the grouper?" Billy asked.

"I do. With hushpuppies and fries."

"And your free drink?"

"Um, I'm not sure."

"The strawberry daiquiris are good. The beer is ice cold."

"I'll have a beer."

"Okay, coming right up." Billy wound his way through the tables to the bar.

She turned her attention to the view. The sun was setting over the harbor, and the sky was turning orange and purple as the sun dipped below the clouds. The breeze picked up, chasing away the remainder of the heat of the day.

"Here you go."

She looked up to see Walker Bodine holding her beer. He was tall. Maybe six feet? With short, dark brown hair and crystal blue eyes that sparkled when he smiled. Which he was doing right now.

"Uh, thank you." What was the owner doing serving up drinks?

"My pleasure. Hope you enjoy the meal." He stepped back and waved to a customer seated a few tables away. "Hey, Bob."

She watched him as he walked away. Long, confident strides. A quick smile and a word to the bartender. Then he disappeared back inside.

The next time she saw Walker—halfway through her delicious meal—he was bussing a table. A boss who jumped in and helped out where needed. Who knew they made bosses like that? Her last boss sat in the back room, smoking endless cigarettes and yelling at people to get to work.

Maybe they needed another waitress here... she wouldn't mind working for a boss like that. Though she'd need to check and see what apartments went for around here. Might be out of her price range this close to the beach. And she really hated to get an apartment too far inland and depend on driving to work every day. Her car wasn't *that* reliable. She usually found apartments where she could walk to work.

She finished her meal and the ice-cold beer. Hadn't had a beer with a meal out at a restaurant in a long time. She usually just ordered water to save on money. She rarely ate out anyway. Much cheaper to eat at home.

She gave Billy the gift certificate to pay for the meal and figured out how much she had left. She'd probably get another meal out of it, and maybe a lunch. Nice. She left a generous tip because she knew how demanding server jobs could be. She looked around to see if she could spy Walker to tell him thanks for the complimentary drink and how much she'd enjoyed the meal. But he was nowhere to be found.

She walked through the inside part of the restaurant and still didn't see him. Disappointed, she headed back down the wharf. She popped into a shop and bought a book to read. She never had time to read, but this week she did. The whole week stretched out gloriously before her.

But she still would like to know who had done all this and couldn't wait to hear what the lawyer had to say tomorrow.

Willow sat outside on the porch of her cottage, sipping on a glass of the white wine that had been delivered. A crisp Pinot Grigio, not too sweet. She'd chilled it while she was at dinner at Jimmy's, and it was a perfect temperature now.

The stars twinkled above her, and a light breeze blew the palm trees, making shadows dance in the moonlight. It was so nice and peaceful here. She relaxed into the rocker and kicked off her shoes, slowly moving the chair back and forth.

She'd managed to do a quick video chat with Eli before he went to bed, and he seemed to be having a great time with his grandmother. Derek had asked about her drive and promised he'd try to talk more later tonight after Eli was in bed. But she knew her husband. He'd be asleep soon, probably on the couch, reading some paperwork from his job. She'd make a point to call him after her meeting at the lawyer's office tomorrow.

It seemed so strange to be sitting here alone. If she were back at home, she'd be doing the dishes and tidying the kitchen. Maybe throwing in a load of laundry. She or Derek would put Eli to bed. Then they'd go into the family room and have a cup of tea, or a glass of wine and talk about their days. No matter how busy they got, that was their time together. But then, after their couple time, both of them would usually tackle work leftover from their jobs.

But here she was alone. And... if she admitted it... enjoying herself in the quiet and solitude. Life had just become such a rush. Constantly moving and hurrying through life. Work, Eli, keeping up with the house. Making sure to spend time with Derek. It was nice to just... sit. Then she immediately felt guilty for the thought because she loved her life with Derek and Eli.

She took another sip of her wine and sucked in a deep breath of the salty air. But there was no reason not to enjoy the quiet while she had it.

CHAPTER 4

Aspen woke up early the next day, anxious to find out what the lawyer had to say. But she had hours and hours to kill before the appointment. After a quick cup of coffee, she pulled on shorts and a t-shirt and headed to the beach. Not many people were out this early, while the sun was just starting to lighten up the sky.

The now-familiar tingle went through her as she saw the blonde lady sitting down near the water's edge, watching the morning awaken. She left the woman to her solitude and headed down the beach in the other direction, letting the waves wash over her feet and stopping to pick up an occasional shell that called to her.

She passed by a woman and a young girl

making a sandcastle. She couldn't remember a single time when her own mother had taken the time to actually sit and play with her. A ridiculous pang of jealously jolted through her at the child's good fortune at having a mother like that. A mother who cared. Who wanted to just sit and play in the sand. How would her life have been different if fate had given her a mother like that?

She turned her head away, erasing the what-ifs, and looked at her watch. She'd better turn around. She still needed to shower and change into something more appropriate for a meeting with the lawyer. What did one wear to a meeting like this? Most of her clothes were casual work clothes. Old and worn at that. But she did have one pair of nice navy pants. She'd search for a top to wear with it that wasn't a t-shirt and call that good enough.

She got back to her cottage, half expecting to see her mother sitting there waiting for her. Maybe her mother would even be happy to see her? But no. No mother waiting for her.

Why was her mother being so mysterious? Confusion wrapped in anger simmered just below the surface. She wasn't sure what her mother was up to, but she didn't feel like playing the game.

Though she had to admit the cottage for a week was nice...

Precisely at ten, Aspen walked into Brown and Bates Law Firm. A perky receptionist greeted her and led her down a hallway to a small conference room. She held her breath, wondering if her mother would be behind the frosted glass door.

As she stepped inside, her eyes widened. No. No sign of Magnolia. But there, sitting at a small table with a smartly dressed man she assumed was Mr. Brown, was the blonde woman from the cottage next to hers.

The man at the end of the table rose and came around to pull out a chair. "Great. Miss Caldwell is here. Aspen Caldwell, this is Willow Sampson."

Willow? She sank into the offered chair and stared at the woman. *Willow?* She shook her head, chasing away some deep memories clambering for attention.

Willow extended her hand. Nails precisely

polished. A silver bracelet dangling from her slender wrist. "Nice to meet you."

She shook her hand and the familiar tingle became more of a shock. She turned to Mr. Brown. "I don't understand. Why are we here? I got that letter from my mother."

"Your mother?" Willow glanced over, confusion clouding her eyes. "I don't understand either."

"Yes, let's get to that." He sat back down and shuffled through some papers in front of him. "You see… and this is awkward and I'm sure will come as a surprise to both of you." He paused dramatically and looked at Willow, then Aspen.

Would he just get to it? She clutched the arms of the chair, holding her breath.

"I'm the executor of your mother's will. I'm working on the details of her estate. Getting things worked out."

Her mother's *will*? Aspen sat back in her chair. Her mother had died? She wasn't sure how she felt about that. How she *should* feel about that. She'd come here pretty much expecting to see her mother again, not to find out she was… gone.

She waited to feel a pang in her heart. Or

any feeling. After all, a person should feel something when they learned their mother had died. But no, there was no twang of pain, no tears. Nothing. It was like reading about a perfect stranger. Which, to be honest, her mother was.

"My mother?" Willow asked softly. "My mother was Geraldine Post."

The lawyer frowned. "Miss Magnolia said she was certain that your adoptive mother would have told you that you were adopted."

"I was adopted?" Willow repeated the words in a whisper, her facing paling.

"She's my sister?" She looked from Willow to Mr. Brown.

"Yes." Mr. Brown bobbed his head.

Memories flooded back through her. Her imaginary friend—*Willow*—that she had for years when she was a young child. Until her mother had told her to quit talking about her. Quit mentioning Willow. Never say her name again.

Aspen turned to stare at Willow. The blonde hair, just like her imaginary friend. So very pretty. And startling blue eyes. Yes, just like her evidently not-so-imaginary friend. "You didn't know you were adopted?"

"No. My mother tried to tell me something as she was… dying. Maybe this was it."

She looked over and took in every detail of this woman. Her sister. She was beautiful, graceful, poised. Dressed in an expensive outfit that probably cost more than Aspen's entire wardrobe. She looked down at her "good" slacks and striped shirt that had seen better days. Her own unruly brown hair was pulled back in a loose ponytail. Not styled smartly like Willow's. Willow was thin and had the look of a woman who worked out regularly, not the look of someone, like her, who carried an extra ten pounds and the only workout she did was standing on her feet for hours waitressing.

"Willow, you were adopted when you were three years old," Mr. Brown continued.

Three. Willow had lived with her and her mother for three years? Willow wasn't an imaginary friend. She was real. Aspen reached out and grasped the edge of the table. "Magnolia gave her up for adoption when she was three?"

"Yes. I don't know the exact circumstances. Miss Magnolia just explained Willow was adopted at three."

But why did her mother keep *her* and give up Willow?

"Magnolia?" Willow's question was barely a whisper.

"Yes, Magnolia. My mother. *Our* mother, I guess. Yours, too. And as you can tell, she had a thing about naming kids after trees." Why was she saying this now? But really, what kind of name was Aspen? She'd always hated her name. What had her parents been thinking? Not that she really remembered her dad. He'd left when she was about five or so.

Her mouth dropped open. *When she was about five or so.* When her mother had given Willow up for adoption.

So many thoughts rattled around her brain. A faint memory of rocking her imaginary friend to sleep in the rocking chair that was way too big. Of pouring her a bowl of cereal for breakfast because their mother had been up late and yelled at them to leave her alone. Only... it hadn't been an imaginary friend like her mother had convinced her.

It had been her *sister*.

She tugged her stare from Willow back to the lawyer. "I thought Magnolia was done surprising me. That she couldn't hurt me again." She purposely relaxed her clenched fists and stared down at her ragged fingernails, nothing like Willow's light pink polished ones. She took a deep breath to steady herself. "But I guess I was wrong."

How could her mother give away her own child?

And why Willow? Why not her? Or both of them, for that matter.

Willow stood up abruptly, knocking her chair over. "I—I have to go." The words came out in a small gasp.

Aspen jumped up and righted the chair, reaching out to touch Willow—her sister's—arm. "Are you okay?"

Willow's eyes widened, and she darted her glance around the room. "I just need... to go."

"Wait... I have more to tell you..." Mr. Brown stood.

"It's going to have to wait a bit." Aspen looked at Willow, concerned about how pale she'd become. "Let's go."

Aspen took Willow's elbow and started to lead her out of the conference room.

"I'll phone and set up another meeting with you," Mr. Brown called after them.

Whatever. Right now, she had to make sure

Willow was okay. She led her down the hallway and out into the fresh air.

"Look, there's a bench in the shade." They walked over to the shade and Willow collapsed onto the brightly painted bench.

They sat in silence for a few minutes. She wasn't sure what to say. Somehow, she felt like she'd failed her sister all those years ago. Letting her mother just give Willow away. Discarding her like an unwanted pet who was too much trouble to keep.

Anger swelled through her. This was the last straw. She tried to remain detached from her mother and memories of her. She never thought she could have a lower opinion of her than she already had… but her mother had outdone herself with this one.

"So… Magnolia… our… mother. She kept you and raised you?" Aspen finally asked, with pain embedded in each word.

"Ah, raised me would be a generous term for her mothering. And she left me alone at seventeen to finish out high school. Took off with her boyfriend of the month and left me with nothing. I haven't heard a word from her since. Well, except for her letter to come here to Moonbeam."

"She left you alone at seventeen? Is that even legal?"

"It wasn't like I was telling anyone she was gone. I just wanted to finish school. Worked a couple of jobs, squeaked by with barely passing grades, and got my diploma. For some reason, I thought that would be important. It's not like any of my jobs have ever asked if I graduated high school." She shrugged.

"What was she like?"

"Magnolia? She was… flighty. We moved all the time. Slipped out in the middle of the night to avoid paying rent. She always had to have a boyfriend. As soon as one left, she'd find another. Stayed out all night pretty often. Sometimes for days. I learned young to only depend on myself."

"I'm sorry… that sounds like a difficult childhood."

"I survived." She didn't want pity. It had been a crummy childhood, but she'd survived it, albeit with scars to her psyche. "How about you? Your adopted parents?"

"I had wonderful parents. Richard and Geraldine Post. We lived about four or so hours from here, up near Jacksonville. I still live there with my husband and son."

"You're married?"

Willow nodded. "Derek and I have been married six years now. And Eli is five."

"And your parents?"

"They're both gone now."

"I'm sorry." She said the words automatically because that's what you said when someone's parents had died.

Like her own mother had...

"So they never told you that you were adopted?"

"No, they didn't. I can't believe they'd hide that from me. Though Mom was struggling to tell me something as she was dying. But she didn't have the strength to finish. It was a little less than a year ago."

"I'm sorry. You must miss her." Again, the automatic reply. "This whole thing is so strange, isn't it?" Aspen let out a long breath of air, trying to send off some of the stress from the morning.

"It is. I feel like everything I thought I knew about my life is... wrong."

"So, how about we go find something to eat? You want to? My treat. Well, Magnolia's treat. The gift certificate to a place called Brewster's on the wharf."

"I could do that. I was too nervous to eat anything this morning. I was so curious about what the lawyer would say." Willow shook her head. "I sure didn't see this coming."

"I didn't either. I actually thought..." She paused and shrugged. "I thought that I'd probably see Magnolia."

"I'm sorry for your loss," Willow said as they stood.

She didn't know how to explain that she had no sense of loss. No twinge of pain. Nothing. And she was too embarrassed to admit that to Willow, anyway.

CHAPTER 5

W illow sat across the table from Aspen at Brewster's. Her *sister*, Aspen. She had a sister. The thought hammered in her brain. The whole morning had unraveled like an unbelievable plot in a movie.

She glanced over at Aspen, who was poring over the menu. She had thick brown hair and kind, honey-brown eyes. And she'd immediately stepped in to help when Willow couldn't breathe after Mr. Brown announced his news and her life had exploded.

The breeze from the harbor blew her menu across the table, and Aspen reached out to catch it and handed it to her.

The words blurred on the page. What did she want to eat? She couldn't concentrate. She barely heard Aspen order and told the server she'd have the same. But she wasn't really sure what she was having. The world swirled around her in slow motion, but she noticed tiny details.

The sun glinting off the water in the harbor. Aspen's hair blowing wildly in the breeze. A thin scar on the back of Aspen's hand.

"You okay?" Aspen asked, interrupting her thoughts.

She looked directly at her sister. "I... I don't know. It was such a shock."

"It was that. Magnolia is great at surprises. Mostly unwanted ones."

"So... do you remember me?"

Aspen's brow creased. "I do. Kind of. Just vague memories. I must have been about five when Magnolia... uh."

"Gave me away?"

"Yes, that. And I had this... imaginary friend. Well, I thought she was imaginary. Her name was... Willow. It must have been you. Eventually Magnolia told me I was too big to have an imaginary friend and to quit talking about you. I hadn't thought about her—*you*—in years."

"Tell me more about Magnolia. What was she like? What did she look like?"

"It's hard to describe her. She was... well, she was a terrible mother. Everything was always about Magnolia. What she wanted to do. How she felt. By the time I was seven or so, I was making the meals... when she would remember to grocery shop. I learned early to squirrel some food away in my room in case she disappeared for a few days so I'd have something to eat."

"That's terrible." Willow could hardly imagine a child living like that. So different from her life. Her parents had centered their lives around her. Her school activities. Her wants and needs.

"I guess your life was different, huh?"

"It was. Mom and Dad were... wonderful." Even if they had kept this secret from her. "I was an only child. They spoiled me."

"Looks like you came out ahead, then." Aspen shrugged.

Maybe she had. But it didn't make the pain any less that her mother had chosen to give her away. After three years. Who could do that? She couldn't imagine what could possibly make her give Eli away. It was unimaginable. The pain would be too great.

"What did she look like? Do you have a

photo?" Suddenly she had this intense desire to see this woman who had given birth to her and then given her way.

"I do. Packed away in one of my boxes. I'll look for it when we get back to the cottages."

"I wonder how Magnolia picked the resort to have us come here?"

"No clue. I don't think I've ever even heard of Moonbeam."

They paused while the server delivered their food. Oh, she'd ordered a chicken salad sandwich. Okay, then.

"It's kind of pretty out here on the wharf, isn't it?" She picked at her sandwich, still not hungry.

"It is. I saw you eating at Jimmy's at the end of the wharf last night."

"You ate there, too?"

"I did."

She set down her fork. "This is all just so unbelievable."

"It is. I guess I should be grateful that Magnolia finally told us the truth. Let us find each other again. I mean, I am happy to meet you. Uh, get to know you." Aspen shook her head, her brown hair swaying back and forth along her shoulders. "Anyway, tell me about your husband. Derek was it? And Eli."

"Ah, Derek is great. He's a fabulous dad to Eli." Guilt stabbed through her about talking about her wonderful, normal life. Aspen's hadn't been anything like hers. "Eli just started school and loves it." She grabbed her purse and pulled out her phone. "Here's a picture of us at the beach a couple of weeks ago."

"Derek is handsome. And Eli? He's a cutie." Aspen handed the phone back.

"How about you? You married? Have someone special in your life?"

Aspen laughed. "No. No one special."

"What do you do? Where do you live?" She had so many questions.

Aspen picked up her coffee and took a sip. "I'm… um… kind of between jobs right now."

She noticed Aspen hadn't really said what she did, nor where she lived, but she didn't press the issue. Though she wanted to throw about a hundred more questions at her sister. Where all had she lived with Magnolia? What was her favorite color? And… how about their father?

"Aspen, what about our father?"

Aspen slowly shook her head. "I don't remember him much. He left when I was about five. About the time Magnolia… you know. Gave you up. I kind of remember him as being fun. Kind. But I remember Magnolia would fight with him. Lots of yelling. Then… one day he was gone."

"You never saw him again?"

"Nope."

"So, he left after I was born?"

"I think so."

So, her father had abandoned her, too. She looked down at her plate, concentrating on her meal. All this new knowledge about her past life. She couldn't quite sort it into a logical order. And the sheer power of the wave of abandonment threatened to drown her.

She took a quick sip of her drink and looked up at Aspen. "I wonder what else Mr. Brown wanted to tell us? I'm sorry that I just kind of jumped up and ran out of the meeting."

"I have no clue. Not sure anything could top this surprise."

"Are you going to stay at the cottage for the week?" Suddenly she was afraid that Aspen would leave now that the truth had been revealed. But then, hadn't she herself planned to leave as soon as she met with the lawyer? And

Aspen didn't seem very willing to talk that much about her life.

Aspen nodded. "I plan to. You staying?"

"Yes, I do believe I will." Her plans to find out what the lawyer wanted and hurry back home disappeared in the breeze. Though she couldn't wait to get back to the cottage and call Derek. She had so much to tell him.

Violet looked across the courtyard and saw the woman in the mint cottage sitting out on the porch. Aspen. That was her name. Such a pretty name.

She looked critically at the cottage. Maybe she should have picked a bit more vibrant shade of mint green. But then, Rob would kill her if she asked him to repaint it. It would have to do like it was. But a tiny bit more cheerful shade of mint green would look better…

Pushing the thought aside, she headed across the courtyard to see if Aspen needed anything.

"Good afternoon. Enjoying your stay?"

Aspen laughed quietly and shrugged, her

brown hair sweeping her shoulders. "I don't even know how to answer that."

Violet frowned. "Do you need something? Everything okay with the cottage?"

She shook her head. "No, it's not that. The cottage is perfect and Moonbeam is a lovely town. It's just... I heard some shocking news today."

"I'm sorry. Are you okay?" People always seemed to open up to her. She was as good at listening to people's problems as a bartender...

"I'm fine. Or I will be. You know Willow in the cottage next door?" Aspen tilted her head toward the yellow cottage.

She'd nailed the perfect shade of yellow on that cottage, if she did say so herself. She leaned against the porch railing, ignoring color choices, and nodded, listening, seeing that Aspen needed to talk.

"I just found out she's my sister."

"Really?" Surprise swept through her. How did someone find out at this age that they had a sister? Imagine how surprised Aspen and Willow must be.

"Really. So let's just say my world has been rocked today."

"I bet." Violet glanced over at Willow's

cottage. "So all the arrangements and deliveries…"

"They were set up by my—I mean *our* —mother."

"Wow, I don't even know what to say. Is your mother coming to see you two?"

"No, that's not happening. According to Mr. Brown, she's… dead."

"I'm so sorry." She reached out and touched Aspen's hand, offering comfort.

Aspen stared down at their hands. "Uh, thanks."

"Are you sure I can't get you anything?" She wished she could do something to help. The woman had just found out her mother had died and she had a sister she hadn't known about. How many shocks could a person take in one day?

"No, I think I'm just going to sit here and… think." Aspen let out a shallow sigh. "Willow went inside. I think she wanted to call her husband. And I promised her I'd look through… uh… I have some boxes in my trunk. I think I might have a photo of our mom. She wants to see it."

"You'll let me know if I can do anything?"

"I'm fine. Really."

Though she didn't look fine. She looked shaken up. But who wouldn't be at hearing news like that? "I'll leave you alone, then."

She turned and crossed the courtyard, through the front office, and into the owner's suite. Rob looked up from the table where he was tapping away on his laptop and frowned. "You okay?"

"Have I ever told you that you're a great brother?" She couldn't imagine just now finding out she had a sibling.

Rob's eyebrows quirked up. "Now I know something is wrong."

She laughed quietly. "You know those women in the mint cottage and the yellow cottage?"

"I guess. Haven't really been paying attention."

"You know. I told you about how all these arrangements had been made and the cottages paid for."

"Okay, right."

"Anyway. They just found out today they're sisters."

Rob pushed back from the table. "Really?"

"Yeah. I don't know all the details, but

evidently their mom arranged all this. But… she's dead now."

"Okay, this is strange." His forehead crinkled into a thoughtful look.

"It is." She eyed him suspiciously. "Now don't go putting this in one of your books."

He laughed. "I make no promises. Anything is up for grabs for my stories."

"I mean it, Robby. You can't go swiping stories from the guests at my cottages."

He grinned and bent his head over his laptop again, tapping away.

CHAPTER 6

Aspen dug around in the boxes in her car and found a couple of photos of Magnolia tucked in the bottom of a box. She was disappointed that Willow never came back out of her cottage all afternoon. She debated on knocking on her door to show her the pictures, but Willow had made it clear that she wanted to be alone.

She didn't want to bother Willow. So she sat out on the porch, waiting for her to come out.

But it didn't happen. And she was a bit tenuous on just what relationship they had now. Okay, they were sisters. But they were strangers, really.

How like Magnolia to throw a bomb into her life and just walk away and let her deal with the cleanup. She shoved thoughts of Magnolia far away and tamped down her anger. Kind of.

By dinner time, her stomach growled, and she decided to walk to Jimmy's again. She'd enjoyed it last night, and to tell the truth, she wanted to be around people. Sitting alone here thinking and stewing over the anger she felt for Magnolia was doing her no good.

With one more glance over at Willow's cottage, she headed out to the wharf. This time, she took a more direct route, proud of herself for starting to figure her way around town. Though why did that matter since she'd only be here this one week?

She strolled down the wharf to the end and entered Jimmy's, standing by the hostess station, waiting for someone to seat her.

"Hey, there. Welcome back." Walker came up and grabbed a menu. "How about I find you a table right by the railing? I think we're in for a great sunset tonight."

She nodded and followed him, surprised and pleased he remembered her. He threaded through the tables, calling out greetings to some of the customers, and stopped by a high-top table with two stools right at the edge of the dining area. She slid onto the stool as he placed the menu on the table.

"I'm Walker, by the way. This is my family's restaurant."

"Nice to meet you, Walker." She didn't tell him she'd already found out his name from the server last night.

He watched her for a moment as if waiting for something. Oh, right. Introduce herself. "I'm Aspen."

He reached out a hand, and she slipped hers into his. A strong grip. Rugged hands.

"Aspen, that's a great name."

She laughed. "If you say so. I always thought it was a strange one. And no way to get a good nickname out of it, either."

He grinned. "Well, Asp probably wouldn't be great. You don't look like a deadly snake. Pen would work, though. But I still prefer Aspen." He glanced away and gave a just a minute sign to a worker across the room, then turned back to her. "Sorry, we're crazy busy tonight and three workers called in sick. The hostess, a server, and a busboy. I'll send a server over as soon as possible."

"Thank you. I'm in no hurry."

He strode away, picking up dirty dishes on a

table as he walked past and stopping to say something to the bartender at the large bar crowded with people at the end of the restaurant. The restaurant hummed with movement and laughter.

Her server came by after a few minutes, and she ordered a local craft beer from the list on a large chalkboard hanging from the rafters of the wooden roof covering the outside eating area. Ceiling fans made lazy circles above her, stirring the humid air.

She sat sipping her beer and perusing the menu. So many choices. She might try the grouper again. Blackened this time. Though fish tacos sounded good, too.

She glanced over and saw Walker leading another group of people out to a table while he frowned at a couple of tables that weren't cleared. Without really thinking what she was doing, she jumped up, grabbed a plastic bin from a nearby counter, and started to clear the tables. It just came naturally to her. What she did.

Walker strode over after seating the group at a large table. "You don't have to do that."

She looked up at him guiltily. Like a kid being caught stealing candy. "I... uh... just thought I could help out a bit. You looked slammed tonight."

"We are, but you're here to enjoy a nice dinner, not clear the tables."

"In real life, I'm a waitress. I guess I wasn't thinking." Though, she wasn't really a waitress now, was she? She had no job. Had no real life to speak of.

He looked at her for a moment. "Want to freelance tonight? And I'll throw in your meal when the crowd thins out. I could use a hostess. Just ask if they want to sit inside or out. There's a table printout where you mark where you're seating people. As you come out and seat them, if you see an empty table, go back and mark it as cleared."

"I can do that."

"Got to make it legal. Let me grab a paper for you to sign. Don't want to run afoul of the local laws."

She signed the paperwork and hurried out to the hostess table, greeting people as they arrived and seating them. Walker popped by and gave her estimates on wait time when the outside tables filled. Soon, she fell into a familiar rhythm. Greet the people, seat the people. Repeat. As the crowd lessened and there was no longer a wait for tables, she also grabbed the plastic tubs and cleared tables, helping in any way she could.

Finally, she was surprised to see it was after nine. And she was ravenous. Walker came up to her and took the menus out of her hand. "Got someone to cover the hostess station now that the rush is over. Come with me. We're going to have some dinner, if you don't mind me joining you."

She followed him out to a table by the railing. She'd completely missed the sunset while she was so busy working.

"Beer? Same as you ordered before but never got a chance to drink?" Walker stood beside the table.

She nodded.

"And what do you want to eat? I'll turn in our orders."

"Grouper again. Blackened?"

"Sure, and I'll get you a salad and hushpuppies, too." Walker headed to the kitchen, and soon returned with two beers. He sat across from her and pushed her frosty glass toward her. He raised his glass to her, and she lifted hers, then took a sip of the ice-cold honey-colored brew. So delicious.

"I really appreciate your help tonight. My mom and dad were out celebrating their anniversary. My sister was helping out in the kitchen. Just a shorthanded night."

"I didn't mind at all." And she hadn't minded. She'd enjoyed it. It felt good to work again. To feel part of the restaurant. Which was silly, because she had just helped out a bit.

He took an envelope out of his pocket and slid it across the table. "Your pay and a share of the tips."

She took the envelope and shoved it in her pocket. "Thank you." The money would come in handy, no matter what amount it was.

"Don't suppose you're looking for a part-time job?" He leaned back in his chair.

"I... uh. I'm just here for the week. Staying at Blue Heron Cottages." But maybe? But a part-time job wouldn't cut it. She needed full-time work. And a place to live she could afford right near work because of her undependable car.

"Too bad. Where's home?"

"Uh, I'm kind of on the road right now. Moving around. Headed to a new job." That was pretty much the truth, right? Kind of the truth? Or maybe more like a wish.

"A nomad, huh? Wouldn't know about that kind of life. Born and raised here. Been working at Jimmy's since I was a boy. Did odd jobs here before I was old enough to officially work here."

A tall blonde woman who looked a lot like Walker came up to the table. "Quite the night, huh? And just on some random Monday night. Figures it would be on a night Mom and Dad were away."

"Tara, this is Aspen. She helped out tonight."

"Ah, you must be the mysterious angel who jumped in and helped us that I heard about. Word has it that you juggled a bazillion things at once. Thank you so much."

"It was nothing." She squirmed in her seat at the praise.

Tara turned to Walker. "So, you offered her a job, right?"

"I did, sis, but she's only in town for the week."

"That's too bad. We could use another hard worker like you." Tara looked over to where a worker was seating another couple. "I better go say hi to the Nelsons. Anyway, thanks, Aspen. You were a real lifesaver tonight."

She blushed at all the compliments as Tara walked away.

"She's right, you know. You were a big help. Dad hates it when things don't run smoothly here. And I'm sure he would have heard about it. Then he'd be sorry he and mom took the night off." Walker shrugged his broad shoulders. "And Tara and I are trying to convince them they don't have to work so hard. That they should take more time off. Hard transition for them, though."

A server brought out their dinners, and she took a bite of the salad with a delicate strawberry vinaigrette dressing, dug into the perfectly prepared grouper, and dunked the hushpuppies into the melted butter. So good. She wasn't used to eating big meals like this. But she managed to eat every last bite.

They sat sipping the last of their beer when an older couple walked up. "We dropped in the office, saw the staffing sheet, and saw how short you were tonight with workers. Why didn't you call us?" The man frowned.

"Because you were taking the night off, remember?" Walker shook his head in exasperation.

"But you needed help," the woman said.

"Mom, Dad, this is Aspen. She jumped in to help tonight. Aspen, these are my parents, Jimmy and Sally Bodine."

"Thank you so much, Aspen. Pretty name, by the way," Sally said with a warm smile.

"It was nothing," she said self-consciously, seriously not used to all the compliments.

Tara walked up. "It wasn't nothing. She was awesome." She laughed. "But don't even bother to suggest it. Walker already asked her if she wanted to work here. She's just here visiting for the week."

"That's too bad." Jimmy gave her a smile as warm as his wife's. "But we appreciate the help tonight. Meals on the house this week."

"You don't have to do that."

"I insist."

"Mom, Dad, you should head home. You promised you weren't even going to check in tonight."

"We didn't promise. You just said we shouldn't." Sally grinned. "But how often have you seen a day that your father doesn't at least pop in and check on things?"

"Good point. But we're still going to try and change that. You know, Tara and I aren't little kids anymore. We're perfectly capable of running the restaurant."

"Of course you are," Jimmy said but didn't look convinced. "Okay, we'll head home. Come on, Sally, we know when we're not wanted." But Jimmy's eyes twinkled as he said the words.

"I should probably go, too." She stood as Walker's parents walked away, stopping to say hi at numerous tables as they headed across the dining area. They seemed to know at least half the customers in the restaurant.

Walker rose from his seat. "I really do appreciate the help."

Suddenly she wanted to come back again. Feel this needed and appreciated again. "If you do get short this week, you could call me. I don't mind coming in again," she offered.

Walker grabbed a pen from his pocket. "Here, write your number on this napkin. I just might do that."

She scribbled her number on the napkin.

"And remember what Dad said. Meals on us this week. As many as you want."

"You don't—"

He held up a hand. "I learned long ago not to argue with Dad. You won't win. Hence you saw that he did pop in tonight after his so-called night off."

"Well, thank you." Wouldn't hurt to be able to save up her money. Free food was always nice. And the Bodines were nice. All of them had been so kind to her.

"How about you walk her home, Walker?" Tara suggested.

"Oh, I'm okay walking alone."

"I could use the chance to get some fresh air." Walker turned to Tara. "Won't be long. I'll be back to help close up."

"Nah, I've got it. You go with Aspen, then head home."

"She's a bossy one, that sister of mine." Walker leaned over and said the words in an exaggerated whisper.

"'Cause I'm always right," Tara tossed the words over her shoulder as she walked away.

Walker led her through the restaurant and out onto the wharf. The lights strung along the wharf twinkled in the night. Crowds had died down, with just a few couples walking by. The stores on the wharf were closed up. "Not much stays open here after about eight at night. Except during the holidays. Then maybe they stay open until nine." He laughed. "Not much of a party town here."

"I love Moonbeam." The words came out unexpectedly. But she did really like the town. The slow pace. The friendly people. Even if the week was filled with surprises.

Like finding out she had a sister.

"It's a great little town. How do you like Blue Heron Cottages? They look like they turned out really nice. The new owner, Violet, bought them from Murphy. He'd really let the place get run down."

"I love my cottage. The whole place is nice. A pretty courtyard. Porches with ceiling fans on each cottage. I've spent a lot of time sitting out on the porch."

"What made you decide to come visit Moonbeam?"

She stopped short. Walker noticed, stopped, and turned back to her. "You okay?"

"Yes… it's just a long, complicated story."

"I have the length of time it takes us to walk to the cottages. More if you need it. I'm a good listener." He gave her an encouraging smile.

She looked at him standing under a lamplight, his eyes shining with sincerity. And who else did she have to talk to about this?

There was no one. Well, there was Willow, but she'd just disappeared on her.

"I just found out about a sister. Like I have a sister I never knew about." The words tumbled out in a rush. "Her name is Willow. This lawyer contacted us and told us this morning when we met at his office. Our mother arranged this little get-together. Willow is staying at the cottages, too. Only she's upset to find out she was adopted and disappeared into her cottage, and I don't want to intrude. And…"

Did any of that make sense?

"That's a lot to learn in one day, isn't it?"

"And I found out my mother is dead." Dead. There, she'd said it. Her mother was dead.

"Oh, I'm so sorry." His eyes filled with sympathy.

She shook her head. "No, I hadn't seen her in years. Not since I was seventeen. So… it's… well, it's strange. I don't know how I feel about anything."

"I'm sure it will take a bit to sort it all out."

She nodded and started walking again. "I guess." Relief swept through her at spilling her news. She'd told Violet earlier about Willow, but not about how she felt about her mother's death. Now Walker knew her whole story. And listened quietly to her spilling it all. He suddenly felt like a friend to her, even though she'd just met him. She didn't get to have a friend very often...

They walked on in silence, but it was a companionable silence. Comfortable. And it felt good not to be so alone.

CHAPTER 7

Aspen answered the door early the next morning to find Violet standing there, a large envelope in her hands. "Sorry to bother you so early. But this just came from Brown and Bates Law Firm. One for you, one for Willow."

She reached for the envelope. Now what? "Thank you."

Violet nodded. "You doing okay?"

She smiled as sincerely as she could, though she wasn't feeling it. "Yes, I'm fine." What a lie that was. She wasn't fine. She couldn't find her footing. Her world was spinning like a merry-go-round, and she couldn't seem to grasp hold of anything to steady herself. Her mother was dead, and she had a sister, but no job and no home.

Violet left, and Aspen pulled out the pages from the envelope with the now dreaded Brown and Bates Law Firm return address. First, a handwritten note from Mr. Brown asking for another appointment for Friday morning. Okay, she could do that. Though she wasn't sure what else he'd have to say. How could he top his last announcement?

She pulled out a cream envelope from the large manila envelope and immediately recognized her mother's handwriting. Her name was scrawled on the front of the envelope. She slowly pried it open and pulled out the page, holding her breath.

Dear Aspen,

I guess you're pretty mad at me right now, huh? Can't say I blame you. And by now you've figured out that your imaginary friend, Willow, wasn't so imaginary. You were so young and kept talking about her after she was gone. As time went on, I convinced you she was just an imaginary friend.

I've made a lot of mistakes in my life. A lot. I'm sure you're listing them off in your mind right now.

. . .

Well, she was. Kind of. Being left alone at seventeen. Being left alone at night, even younger than that. Going hungry. Cramming her feet into shoes two sizes too small. Always worrying that someone would find out her mother had disappeared for days... sometimes weeks... at a time. And—the big one—having a sister who was given away. She turned back to the letter.

I thought I was doing the right thing giving Willow up for adoption. She was such an easy child. So beautiful with her blonde hair and bright blue eyes. Quiet. I just knew someone would want her. The adoption agency said you'd be harder to place because you were older.

I could barely keep you and me in food and clothes. Then Willow came along. I just didn't know what to do.

Anyway, I hope you take this week to get to know your sister better. You were inseparable when you were young. You cried for months, begging for her to come back. I'm sorry that I split you two apart, but what's done is done. Maybe you two can find a way to be sisters again.

Magnolia

. . .

She didn't know if she wanted to crumple the letter up into a ball, or burn it, or what. She was so over her mother throwing her curveballs. Upending her life like she had the million times they'd snuck out in the middle of the night and moved to a new town states away. Starting a new school. Always struggling to keep up and figure out what she was supposed to know at whatever grade at the new school. Never any advance warning that they were going to leave. No chance to say goodbye to any friends she made. So, after a while, she'd learned not to make friends. It was easier that way.

There had actually never been a person in her life that she could call her best friend. Or even a close friend.

But now there was Willow. Finally, she'd have some family.

But first, Willow would have to come out of her cottage…

Willow knew she was being a scaredy-cat. She'd been hiding out in her cottage. Trying to process everything the lawyer had said yesterday. Thankful for the basket of snacks that had been delivered, she'd just munched on a few items for dinner last night. She knew she was avoiding going out so she wouldn't see Aspen. Because seeing Aspen just reminded her that her parents had kept a very important secret from her. They'd never told her the truth. That they, in fact, weren't her birth parents.

Then there was the fact that her own birth mother had given her away.

As all this sank in, she just felt more and more off-kilter. Ungrounded.

Even after talking to Derek for hours last night, she couldn't quite wrap her mind around everything she'd found out yesterday. Everything that had blown her whole life up. Everything she'd thought she knew was just a mirage.

She didn't like that. Her life was all planned out. Carefully organized. Lists of when things needed to be done. Checking items off, one by one. She liked... sameness. Continuity. Her carefully crafted life.

But now nothing was the same. Her parents had lied to her. All her life. Lied. If they could lie to her, the people she trusted most, who else could?

Certainly not Derek...

... or could he?

She sat in a chair, staring down into the cup of coffee she was holding. She couldn't just hide out inside all day, could she?

She rose at the sound of a knock at the door. Probably Aspen wanting to talk. She wasn't sure she was ready for more talking. She set the cup down with a sigh and went to open the door.

Violet stood there holding a large manila envelope. "This got delivered for you."

"Okay. Thank you." She reached out and took the envelope, noticing the Brown and Bates Law Firm return address.

"Do you need anything else?" Violet looked at her closely.

You mean like how I want my old life back? How I want to hide in bed from the truth? But she didn't say any of that. "I'm fine, thank you," she lied.

Violet looked like she wanted to say something else, but just nodded and walked away, heading back to the front office.

Willow stared at the letter in her hands, not really wanting to open it. She set it down on the counter—ignoring it—poured another cup of coffee, and walked away to look out the window. Sunshine streamed down outside and fluffy blue clouds dotted the sky. A beautiful day beckoning her. Yet... she didn't want to go out. Didn't want to see people. She glanced back over at the envelope mocking her. And she certainly didn't want any more surprises.

She finished the cup of coffee and realized the last sip of it was cold. How long had she just been standing at the window?

She walked over to the sink and rinsed the cup, avoiding looking at the envelope. Until she couldn't. With a sigh, she grabbed it and ripped it open. A letter from Mr. Brown requesting another appointment on Friday. And another envelope tucked inside with flowing handwriting on the front. She ran her fingers over her name. Willow. With trembling hands, she opened the envelope.

My dear Willow,

You were the most beautiful child. I can still picture your face in my mind. I kept one photo of you from when you were about two. Your blonde hair and clear blue eyes. You were wearing a pink dress in the photo. I'm sure Aspen had dressed you. She usually did. She always somehow managed to find a clean outfit for you.

I wasn't the best mother, as I'm sure Aspen has told you by now. And I don't know how to say how sorry I am that you and Aspen were split up. I just couldn't do it anymore. Aspen was fairly independent by then, but you were young and needed so much care.

I hope you had a good life with your new parents. I did meet them once. They seemed like good people and they really wanted a child.

I should say that I'm sorry for giving you up for adoption, but I'm not really sure if I am. I was a terrible mother to Aspen. And by placing you with your new parents, I hoped I was giving you a better chance at life than our barely scraping by existence.

I've made mistakes. Many of them. But I'm not sure that giving you a chance at a normal, good life was one of them.

I hope you and Aspen can get to know each other a little better this week. She loved you so.

My lawyer will have my last letter for you on Friday.

M

She stared at the page, no longer seeing the words. Her mother didn't regret giving her away, it seemed. Magnolia didn't think it was a *mistake* to give her away. Well, fine then. She didn't need this Magnolia person anyway. Didn't need to know about her. Didn't need to see a photo of her. It was better if she couldn't even picture her. She was gone anyway. Died without giving Willow a chance to meet her.

Too little, too late.

She crumbled the paper into a ball and tossed it across the room, looking around wildly. She needed to get away. She was done with all this and wanted to get back to her simple, well-planned life. So much for telling Aspen she was staying the week. She wasn't. She was leaving. Going home. Back to her family. Her real family. Not this surprise one.

She rushed into the bedroom and grabbed her suitcase, throwing her clothes into it. She paused at the sound of a knock at the door. Debating on answering it, she stood with a blue dress in her hands, half-folded. With a long sigh, she set the dress on the bed and headed to answer the door.

She tugged it open, not surprised to see Aspen standing there. "Hey, guess you got a letter, too," Aspen said, her face filled with concern.

"I did." She tilted her head toward the ball of paper on the nearby counter.

"Do you want to talk? Or?"

No, she didn't want to talk. She wanted to

avoid this whole thing. Pretend it didn't happen. Go back home.

"I found a photo of Magnolia." Aspen held out a creased photograph.

Willow shook her head. "No, I don't need to see it. See her. I just… don't."

Aspen nodded and shoved the photo into her back pocket. "You look pale. You okay?"

"I'm okay." That was a big, fat lie. "I'm just packing my suitcase."

"You're leaving?" Aspen's eyes widened. "You're not staying the week? Staying to hear what the lawyer has to say on Friday?"

"No, I think I'm done with surprises. He can call me, or send me a letter, or something."

"Oh, I see." A look of disappointment flashed across Aspen's face, but she quickly covered it up.

"It's all a bit much, isn't it? I just need… to go home."

"A bit much? That's like the biggest understatement ever." Aspen paused. "But… I was hoping to get to know you better. Spend some time with you. Make up for lost time. We have the cottages for the week…"

She wavered then. Wanting to run away from all of this. It would be easier that way.

Because what if she got to know Aspen? What difference did that make? They were just going to go back to their separate lives. Apart. Not really knowing each other like real sisters who had grown up together.

"I need to get home." To run, hide. Her thoughts mocked her.

Aspen nodded. "If that's what you need. Maybe later, after you get used to all this... Maybe we could meet up again."

She bobbed her head. "Yes, maybe we could do that." But her words sounded empty, even to her.

"I..." Hurt flashed in Aspen's eyes as a look of sadness swept over them. "Well, goodbye then," Aspen said softly, looking intently at her as if memorizing each feature.

"Goodbye." Guilt stabbed at her as she stepped back and closed the door. Closed it against the pain. The shock. Yes, she was a scaredy-cat. And she didn't care right now. She wanted to go back to her real life and pretend all this hadn't happened.

CHAPTER 8

Aspen went back to her cottage, feeling
strangely alone. And feeling… rejected.
Yes, that's what she was feeling. She wanted to
get to know Willow. Find out about this sister
she had. But Willow? She wasn't interested in
that. Not interested in getting to know her. Not
interested in hearing about Magnolia.

Okay, the not wanting to know about
Magnolia, she got that. Magnolia had given her
away.

But *she* hadn't done anything to Willow.
She'd been a victim in all this, too. And
yesterday, for a brief moment, she'd thought
she'd finally found family. Real family. Or at
least had a chance at it.

But Willow had snatched that dream from her. She was packing up and leaving her, just like Magnolia had.

She tamped down her disappointment and... anger. Yes, there was anger there, too. Just another rejection in a long line of rejections. Her dad leaving, her mom leaving. Then a series of broken relationships with men until she pretty much gave up dating.

Now, a sister who didn't want her in her life.

Fine then.

She was fine with that. Just fine.

She'd always been a loner. She could still be one.

Only... she felt so... *incredibly* alone.

She wrapped her arms around herself, staring out into the courtyard. Waiting to see Willow load up her car and leave. One last glimpse of her. How pathetic was that?

Her phone rang, and she snatched it off the table.

"Hey, it's Walker."

"Hi."

"So, I was wondering. If you're not too busy... Would you like to cover the hostess station again for the lunch shift?"

"I'd love to." The words rushed out. She

would love to. It was infinitely better than standing here feeling sorry for herself. She'd just keep herself busy until Friday. Find out what Mr. Brown had to say. Then leave at the end of her week's stay. She'd seen the price of a night's stay here at the cottages, and she'd never be able to afford even one extra night here. So, she'd enjoy the cottage while she could. At least she had a roof over her head.

"That would be great," Walker said enthusiastically.

"I'll head over there now."

"Okay, see you soon. And thank you."

She convinced herself that it was just about keeping busy. It didn't have anything to do with seeing Walker again. Seeing if he still felt like a friend today or if it was just some kind of magic last night when she'd spilled everything to him. But anyway, if she went to Jimmy's, maybe she wouldn't feel this mind-numbing loneliness. She'd be surrounded by people.

She set the phone down and went into the bedroom, digging through clothes. She pulled off her faded shorts and t-shirt and finally found a decent pair of slacks and a clean polo shirt. That looked nice enough.

She left the cottage and headed through the

courtyard. She paused at the edge and allowed herself one last look back at Willow's cottage. "Goodbye, Willow," she whispered as disappointment seared through her.

She resolutely turned her back on the cottage and headed toward the wharf.

Tara greeted her when she got to Jimmy's. "Oh, good. You're here. I swear, we've been having the worst luck with employees. One is out on maternity leave, one got called away because their mom was sick out of town somewhere. Oh, and one has the flu. We're not usually this shorthanded."

"I'm glad to help." She didn't bother to say that she needed the money or that it was keeping her busy instead of stewing over Willow.

She took over the hostess station and started seating people. It was easier today. She'd memorized which table was which and soon figured out who was waiting on which tables so she could spread out the load. Walker came up after she'd been working about forty-five minutes.

"There you are. Tara said you were here. I've been working in the kitchen. The special today is chili, and well... I'm the official chili maker at Jimmy's."

"Good to know."

"You should try it. I swear, it's the best chili you'll ever taste." His eyes sparkled as he bragged.

Tara passed by. "And he's so modest, too." She rolled her eyes.

Aspen laughed, enjoying their sibling teasing and ignoring the fact that she'd never have that with Willow. "I'll have some when my shift is over."

Lunchtime sped by, and by mid-afternoon she was seated at a table and enjoying a large bowl of chili. Which she had to admit was excellent. Just spicy enough. With a sprinkle of cheese on top, then sour cream, then tiny round crackers.

Walker slid onto the seat across from her. "Well, was I right? Best chili ever?" He raised an eyebrow, waiting for her answer.

"I confess, it ranks up there with the best."

"Only ranks up there? Doesn't top any other bowl ever?" His lips quirked up in a lopsided smile. A really nice lopsided smile.

"Okay, okay. It really is the best chili ever."

"Ah, ha. I knew it." He laughed. "Now is confession time. It's my grandmother's recipe. Only my family is convinced I make it better than any of them do. Or... maybe, it's just that they don't want to have to make it, so they tell me I'm the best." He shrugged, grinning. "Anyway, I appreciate the help today. Too bad you're only here for the week. We're going to be shorthanded for a couple more weeks until Kristy gets back from maternity leave."

"I can help all you need this week," she offered. "Always willing to earn some extra cash."

"I figured you'd be busy with Willow."

"She... ah..." She stared down at the almost empty bowl of chili, then looked up into his kind eyes. "She left today." She ignored the squeeze in her heart.

"Oh?"

"I was hoping to get to know her, but she wanted to go home. I think it was all too much for her. And she has family at home. A husband, a son." She shrugged, trying to look like it was no big deal her sister had left her.

"I'm sorry. I'm sure you were hoping to get to know her a bit better."

"I was, but… it is what it is. Everybody deals with things in their own way."

"I'd never admit this to Tara and would deny it if anyone ever insisted I said this, but a sister is a pretty cool thing to have."

It looked like she'd never get to know whether it was a cool thing or not. "You're a lucky guy."

"I am. And I'm really sorry she left." He reached over and touched her hand, just momentarily. The lightest of touches.

But she felt the connection. Then, just like that, his hand was gone, and he jumped up from his seat. "So, were you serious about working more this week?"

"Sure was."

"Tomorrow dinner shift? Starts at four p.m."

"I'll be here." Too bad he didn't ask her to work tonight, because she would have stayed and worked another shift. This keeping busy thing was much better than sulking.

"See you tomorrow then." He headed away. The black Jimmy's t-shirt he wore strained across his broad shoulders, and his long, tanned legs stretched out of well-worn khaki shorts. She looked down at her hand where he'd touched her. By the time she looked up again, he'd disappeared inside. She slid off the barstool, reluctant to leave. She'd take the long way back to the cottages. She was in no hurry to get back and sit there all alone.

CHAPTER 9

Willow slowly packed up her things, carefully folding them to fit in her suitcase. She had a system for packing. Organized. She went to the closet and grabbed another cotton dress she'd brought and folded it precisely, making sure it wouldn't get wrinkled. Though she'd probably pop everything into the laundry when she got home anyway. She always did that when she got back from trips.

She flipped the top of the suitcase closed and zipped it up. There. All ready. She'd go over and tell Violet she was leaving. Turn in her key. Then she'd head out. She should make it home before dark.

But she sank down on the bed, staring at the suitcase. She bought it after doing careful research. It had good reviews. A dark charcoal gray that didn't show dirt, and the wheels worked perfectly. She'd bought a set. A large suitcase, a medium one, and an overnight size. She'd packed the medium one for this trip.

Why was she sitting here obsessing over her suitcase?

She wanted to go home, she did. But this tiny part of her brain mocked her, asking if she didn't want to stay and get to know Aspen. And she could still picture the look in Aspen's eyes when she said she was leaving. Guilt swept through her again.

A knock sounded, and she pushed off the bed, hoping it wasn't Aspen. She couldn't face another goodbye with her. She'd made up her mind, right?

Crossing to the front room, she pulled the suitcase with her and set it in the middle of the room. A promise that she was leaving. She tugged the door open.

"Derek!" She threw herself into his arms.

He held her tight, stroking her hair while she clung to him. This. This is what she needed. Where she felt at home. Familiar. Safe.

He finally released her and smiled down at her. "Hey, babe."

"Hey, babe, yourself. What are you doing here?" She grabbed his hands and pulled him inside the cottage.

"I was worried about you. You sounded so upset."

"But work…"

"Took a few days off. And Mom is watching Eli. I just thought you could use some moral support. Or a shoulder. Or I'll just listen. Anything you need. I couldn't let you deal with this alone." He stepped inside and spied her suitcase. "Were you leaving?"

She nodded. "I just packed up. I was headed home."

"We can go home if that's what you want. But are you *sure* that's what you want? What you need?"

Leave it to Derek to ask the tough questions. She reached up and touched his face, and he captured her hand in his. She smiled then. "I don't know what I want. But I do know that I'm so glad to see you."

"How about you let me change into some shorts and we'll go for a walk on the beach. Talk if you want. Or just walk."

"That sounds wonderful."

He disappeared into the bedroom, and she

stood by the window, looking out. The sense of panic began to recede a tiny bit. Derek was here. Part of her organized, carefully planned, familiar life. She needed that. The sameness. The continuity.

Derek came out of the bedroom dressed in shorts and a New Orleans t-shirt from their trip to the French Quarter last year when they'd gotten away for a long weekend and Derek's mom had watched Eli. It seemed like an eternity and a different life ago.

"Ready?" he asked as he settled a ball cap on his head.

"I'm ready." She slipped her hand in his, and they headed out into the sunshine, across the warm white sand, to the water's edge. The tension inside her slowly began to seep away in the sunshine and warm breeze.

Aspen wandered along the streets, then cut over to the beach. When she hit the sand, she slipped off her shoes and walked to the water's edge, letting the waves sweep over her feet. She looked out to sea and watched a pair of gulls flap in rhythm as they flew past. Even the gulls had friends or family...

Wow, what a pity party she was having today. It was kind of ridiculous. Because it wasn't like much had changed. So, she'd found out she had a sister. But Willow was leaving. She was still the same person she'd been before she found out about Willow. So why was she so much lonelier now?

She shook her head, clearing her thoughts. Pity was not a good look. She'd never let herself wallow in her circumstances before. She always just picked herself up and moved on. Which was what she would do now. She'd enjoy every moment in her cute little cottage. Enjoy earning some money at Jimmy's.

Enjoy spending time with Walker... though she knew her rules about making friends. *Don't make any.*

Because come Sunday, she'd move on. Find a new place to live, a new job. So... no friendship with Walker. It was in the rulebook. With that decided, she headed down the beach toward the cottage, enjoying the sunshine and fresh air, her mood slightly improving with each step.

She remembered going to the beach once with Magnolia. It was in California. She was maybe about ten, and they were on their way to yet another town. They'd found a long pier that stretched way out into the ocean, with a diner on the end of it. They had burgers and malts there. She remembered that. Just her and Magnolia. No boyfriend at the time for her mom. Then they walked down the long pier back to the sandy beach and stepped into the water. A big wave had rushed up and caught them unaware. A cold wave. Dashing frigid water over them. Magnolia had grabbed her hand and stood, water flowing from her hair and her clothes clinging to her. She threw back her head and laughed. "Never let it be said that your momma didn't take you to see the Pacific Ocean."

They'd gone back to their car, slipped on dry clothes, and headed down the highway. But she remembered that moment. When her mom had been happy and carefree. Just the two of them. A few special hours. But within a couple of days, they'd found a new town to live in and Magnolia had hooked up with some bartender. And life went on in its predictable, unending way. Struggling at a new school. Until, once again, they disappeared in the middle of the night.

"Aspen?" She looked up from her memories at the sound of her name.

Willow stood in front of her with a tall man by her side.

"I thought you left." She eyed the two of them, not really sure if she was seeing things. Had she just wished Willow back into existence like her imaginary friend?

"I... I decided to stay. Aspen, this is Derek, my husband."

Derek reached out a hand. "Great to meet you, Aspen."

She put her hand in his, surprised at its strength and the genuine warmth in his words. "Nice to meet you."

"I came and surprised Willow." He looked down at Willow and smiled at her. A smile that said he cared about her. That she was special to him.

"And after talking to Derek, I've decided that it's silly to leave. It was... cowardly." Willow looked directly at her. "I was running away. Back to my safe, predictable world. But... that's not really what I want. I want to get to know you better. Stay here. Find out what Mr. Brown has to say on Friday."

"Oh." She didn't really know how to respond. She didn't want to get her hopes up, only for Willow to change her mind again.

Willow reached out and took her hand. "I do want to get to know you. Find out everything about you. Your life. Everything. I'm sorry I was so…" She shrugged her slender shoulders. "Anyway. I'm here for the week. I promise."

She nodded.

"So how about I take you two to dinner tonight? My treat," Derek said. "Unless you two want to go alone."

"Ah, no. I mean yes." She swung her glance between Derek and Willow. "I'd like to go to dinner, and I'd love to get to know you, too. Let's all go."

"How about Jimmy's? It was really good the other night," Willow suggested.

She laughed. "That's a great idea. They have really good food." She didn't bother to explain she'd eaten there last night and today for lunch. Or that she'd worked two shifts there. She sure didn't mind going back again. The food was great. That was all it was. The food.

Because rules. The no-friends rule.

"Perfect." Willow smiled. "We were just going to head back to the cottage. Mind if we join you on your walk?"

"That would be fine." She fell into step beside them. Derek holding Willow's hand as they strolled down the beach. And so began the non-stop questions between her and Willow.

CHAPTER 10

They got back to the cottages and sat on Willow's porch, still asking endless questions. Violet waved at them from across the courtyard, and Aspen waved back. Derek made them tea, and they sat talking some more. Aspen marveled at the differences in their lives. Willow had had every advantage. Loving parents. Fancy clothes. A college education her parents paid for. A truly nice husband, and she'd bet that Eli was a great kid. She'd seen a photo of their house… a wonderful, big, rambling house with an actual picket fence. Willow had the perfect life.

She tried to keep some of the details of her own life hidden. She didn't mention that she had no place to live after this week, or the fact she had no job. She alluded to working at a restaurant. That was close enough to the facts. She didn't want Willow to think she was some kind of loser.

And she wasn't a loser. She was a hard worker. Always had been. She'd just had a really long string of bad luck.

Willow finally glanced at her watch. "Oh, look how late it is. Are you hungry? We should probably head to Jimmy's."

"I'll drive," Derek offered.

"Or we could walk." She was kind of getting into this walk all over town thing. But then, maybe they weren't walking type people.

"Sounds like a plan. Meet you in five minutes and we'll head out?" Willow stood.

She went to her cottage, debated changing clothes, but really had nothing appropriate to change into. This outfit would have to do. Besides, Jimmy's was a very casual place to eat. She brushed her hair and decided to pull it back with a silver clip. Then with a quick look in the mirror, she decided it wouldn't be a bad idea to add a touch of eye shadow and a hint of blush. And an almost nude shade of lipstick. Why was she doing this? To compete with Willow's stunning looks... or because she might see

Walker? Shaking her head at herself, she went outside.

Willow and Derek were standing there waiting. Derek had his arm wrapped around Willow's waist. Seriously, they looked like they should be in some kind of fashion magazine.

"I'm all set." She ignored her worn outfit that suddenly made her feel dumpy and pasted on a smile.

They headed out to the street and Willow laughed. "Which way? I don't know my way around town yet."

"Come on. It's this way." She led the way down the sidewalk, cut across to Magnolia with its shops and restaurants, then over to the wharf, feeling *almost* like a native.

Tara greeted them at the hostess station. "Aspen, welcome back."

"Thanks, Tara. This is my sister, Willow, and her husband, Derek."

"Nice to meet you two. I've got a table by the water. Almost sunset and it looks like it's going to be a great one."

They followed Tara to their table, and Aspen glanced around the dining area, looking for Walker. No sign of him. She didn't know if that was good or bad.

Don't forget the no-friends rule.

She and Derek ordered glasses of a local craft beer, and Willow ordered white wine. They sipped their drinks while they looked through the menu.

"Hey, Aspen. Tara said you were here." She spun around in her seat to see Walker standing there, a friendly smile on his face. Her heart beat in double time.

No, it didn't. "Hi, Walker," she said with enforced calmness.

"So, Tara said this is your sister and her husband." He sent her a questioning look. Of course, he did. Just this afternoon, she told him Willow had left.

"Ah, yes. Willow, Derek, this is Walker. His family owns Jimmy's."

Derek reached out and shook Walker's hand. "Great to meet you. The girls say the food here is great. Looking forward to it."

"Hope you enjoy your meals," Walker said as he waved to an older couple entering the dining area. "I'll stop by later and check on you." He hurried off to greet the couple.

"So, they all know your name here?" Willow cocked her head and looked at her.

"Ah, I've eaten quite a few meals here… and

I worked a couple of shifts. They're short-staffed right now." She shrugged, not mentioning that she could use the money. It was obvious that Willow didn't have to think about money. But she was self-conscious about just how often she did have to count her pennies. Like always. Willow would probably never understand that. But she didn't want her sister's pity, so she kept her circumstances to herself.

"I didn't know you'd worked here." Willow's eyes widened. "Wasn't this a week of vacation for you?"

"I guess I don't do vacations very well." She forced a wide smile, hoping to throw her off this line of questioning.

The server came up to take their orders and rescued her from the conversation. By the time they ordered, the sun was starting to show off in a brilliant display of colors, illuminating the clouds and shimmering off the water.

"Wow, that's a sunset to remember," Derek said. "Why don't you two stand at the railing and I'll get a photo of you."

"Ah… okay." She got up and self-consciously stood beside Willow. Painfully aware that her beautiful sister was dressed in nice slacks, a blouse that perfectly highlighted her blue eyes, and designer shoes. And here she was in worn pants she'd picked up years ago at Target, a shirt that she'd had to sew up the side seam just a few weeks ago, and no-name canvas tennis shoes.

"Perfect," Derek said as he took their photo. He turned the phone to show them. "Want me to send it to your phone?"

She nodded and gave him her number. A ding and the photo appeared. She now had a photo of herself... with her sister. The striking difference between the two of them was not lost on her as the photo faded into her phone.

They ate their meals, and Willow regaled her with stories of Eli's antics. He sounded like a fun-loving, energetic boy, and it was obvious that both Derek and Willow were proud of him. Willow's eyes shone as she talked about him.

As they finished their dinner, Walker came back to the table. "Did you enjoy your meals?"

"Best grouper I've ever had." Derek leaned back and patted his stomach.

"We've got key lime pie. Would you like to try some?"

"I would." Derek nodded. "How about you girls?"

They both nodded.

"You want to join us?" Willow asked.

Now why had her sister done that? She looked quickly at Willow, then at Walker.

"Don't mind if I do. Things are tapering off here. Four pieces of key lime pie coming up." Walker left, and she watched his long strides as he crossed the distance.

"Why did you ask him to join us?" She frowned at Willow.

"Because he seems like a nice guy? And I want to ask him more questions about Moonbeam. Why do you think Magnolia picked Moonbeam for us to meet?"

"That, I don't know."

Soon he was back with their desserts and slipped onto the seat next to her. She took a bite of the tart and tangy pie. "This is really good."

"Another one of my grandmother's recipes. Only I don't let them rope me in to making all the pies. We serve it every day." Walker grinned at her.

"The whole meal was delicious. Your family runs a wonderful restaurant," Willow said.

"Why, thank you. Love to hear that."

"And Jimmy?" Willow asked as she took a bite of the pie.

"That's my father. He opened the restaurant years ago."

"His mom works here, too. And you met his sister, Tara, when we came in."

"So the whole family works here? That's nice." Willow smiled. "I guess you're all close."

"Yep. We are. We have our skirmishes, but as a rule, we all get along great."

"Derek comes from a large family. Two brothers and a sister. But I'm an only—"

Willow stopped and looked at Aspen, a rueful expression covering her face. "Well, I *thought* I was an only child. But I guess I'm not."

"That's really great that you two found out about each other," Walker said.

"It is. And they've talked non-stop all afternoon and through dinner." Derek laughed.

"We have a lot of catching up to do," Willow insisted.

"We do." She nodded in agreement, glad that she was finally getting this chance to get to know Willow better. Even if it did bring out the fact that they and their lives were polar opposites.

"Have you always lived in Moonbeam?" Willow asked.

"I have. So have my parents. All born and raised here. My grandparents moved here in their twenties."

"It seems like a nice town."

"It is. Friendly people. Nice size. Good food." He grinned. "It's really all I know, so I can't compare it to much."

Tara dropped by the table. "Hey, Walker. Why don't you knock off now and head home? I've got this. I'll close. And Dad is still here in the office, too, if I need anything."

"Sounds good to me." He turned to her. "Mind if I tag along with you guys walking home? It's on the way to my house."

"Sure."

They all headed out, down the wharf, stopping occasionally to look in some of the store windows, not that any of the shops were open this late. Then they headed down Magnolia and over to the cottages.

When they got to the cottages, Willow paused at Aspen's cottage. "I'm exhausted. I think we'll call it a night."

"Thanks for dinner, Derek."

"My pleasure. We'll see you tomorrow?"

Willow and Derek crossed to the neighboring cottage, hand in hand, and slipped inside. She turned to Walker, expecting him to head out. Instead, he leaned against the porch railing. "You tired?" he asked.

"Not really."

"Mind if I stay awhile?"

"No, that would be nice. Would you like a glass of wine?" She hadn't opened the expensive-looking bottle of red wine that had come in the basket.

"Sounds good."

She went inside, opened the bottle, and poured two glasses. Then as she was heading back out, she paused to glance in the mirror. Setting down the glasses, she redid the silver clip in her hair. That would have to do. She grabbed the glasses again and headed outside.

Walker was sitting on the porch swing. He patted the seat next to me. "Come join me?"

She walked over and sat beside him, handing him his glass. Walker pushed with his long leg, setting the swing into a gentle swaying motion.

"So, I see that Willow decided to stay."

"She did. Derek came to surprise her. I think she just needed... I don't know. Some stability? Something familiar? Anyway, he seems like a really nice guy."

"He does. And you and Willow? Things going good between you two?"

"I think so. It's kind of strange getting to

know her. Her life is… really different from mine."

"How so?"

She wasn't sure how to answer that. She didn't really want to say something like Willow was beautiful, accomplished, had a wonderful husband, son, and home. A great job. And she was—and had—none of those.

"We just have different lives." There. She'd leave it at that.

"So, you never said where you lived."

"A bunch of towns. I don't stay in one place very long."

"And where are you headed now?"

She couldn't quite admit that she had no idea. "A town up north in Georgia." Not really a lie. She *had* considered looking for a job up on the Georgia coastline. Maybe up near Savannah. She'd heard it was beautiful up there.

"We'll miss you here."

She looked at him quickly, unsure how to take his comment. He probably just meant that they needed her to work at Jimmy's.

"So, I was wondering. Do you have any plans for Thursday evening?"

"Why, you want me to work the lunch shift?"

He laughed. "No, actually, we're having a barbecue for Tara's birthday. Family and a few friends. Starts at five. We hopefully have Jimmy's covered, but I'm sure Dad will sneak away and check on things.

"Are you sure? I wouldn't be intruding?"

"Are you kidding? Tara can't stop talking about how great you are. Swears you're the best worker I've ever hired."

She blushed and took a sip of her wine, not knowing how to respond to that.

"So, you'll come?"

She nodded, wondering what she could get for Tara that wouldn't cost too much but would be a nice gift.

"Great. Tara will be thrilled. So will Mom. She's pretty much a fan of yours now, too."

She didn't know how she'd gotten so swept up in the Bodine family, but she liked it. But then she reminded herself of the rule. Don't make friends. But it was too late now to back out of the birthday party. She'd already said she'd go. Well, she'd just go for a little bit. It would be okay. Wouldn't it?

"So are you enjoying staying here at the cottages?"

"I am. They are great. And I've managed a

walk on the beach every day. Love going to sit on the beach and watch the sunrise."

"Oh, an early morning person, are you?"

"I am. I love that time of day when the world is waking up."

He smiled at her. He had such a nice smile. "That's a great way of putting it. Me? I'm not so much on early rising. I'm a late-night person. Which comes in handy because I put in some late nights at Jimmy's closing up. We're trying to get my parents to leave early now, but even if Mom will sometimes go home early, it's almost impossible to get Dad to leave early." He shrugged. "But Jimmy's has been their whole life for a lot of years. Well, the restaurant and Tara and I."

"I think it's wonderful that you all work together. That you have such a tight-knit family."

"You think that you and Willow will become close?"

"I don't know. We kind of missed our opportunity for that when we were younger and Mom gave her away." And Willow's life was so different from her own.

"That must be really hard for Willow to take. Knowing her own mother gave her away."

She frowned. "I'm sure it is." Though she still wasn't sure that Willow didn't get the better end of things. Magnolia had been a really poor mother at best.

"You two have time to get to know each other now. You could plan regular visits."

"Maybe. It's all kind of new. And Willow and Derek have their own friends and family. Derek's big family. They do a lot of family stuff with them." She didn't know if they would really want to incorporate her into all of that. Plus, she doubted she'd fit in. Not with rich people who drove fancy cars and wore expensive clothes.

"I'm glad you'll at least have the chance. Everyone should have family."

Maybe. But she wasn't sure that Willow thought of her as family. Not grown-up-together real family.

He took the last sip of his wine. "I should probably head out. Let you get some shut-eye. I hear you're an early riser." He grinned.

Suddenly, she didn't want him to leave. It was nice just sitting here talking to him. "I'm still not tired. Would you like another glass of wine?"

He looked at her for a long moment. "Yeah, maybe a short pour."

She got up and went inside, surprised she'd gotten up the nerve to ask him to stay. She poured two small glasses of wine and returned to the swing.

"It's a nice night tonight. Not too humid. Good breeze. Love nights like this here in Moonbeam." Walker looked up at the sky. "And look at those stars. Millons of them. You can really see them out here near the beach."

She glanced up, taking in the night sky, and turned to Walker. "It is a nice night." And she wasn't just talking about the beautiful sky and the nice weather. She totally ignored the nagging thought in her mind.

Don't make friends.

Totally ignored it.

They sat in the swing, chatting about this and that. Sipping their wine. Easy conversation. The slow motion of the swing. A feeling of contentment wrapped around her like a cozy quilt. This day that started out so lousy had turned into a really special day that she'd remember for a very long time.

CHAPTER 11

Aspen snuck out early the next morning and settled on the beach to watch the sunrise. The sky was just beginning to lighten. The waves rolled slowly on the shore, not much more motion than a lake in the still air. The sand was cool against her bare legs, though the weather report said they were in for an unseasonably hot day today.

She looked up at the sound of someone approaching. An older lady with spry steps walked up to her. "Another early riser." Her warm smile spread across her face. "Mind if I join you? Or would you prefer to be alone?"

"No, sure. Join me."

The woman sat down in the sand beside her. "I'm Rose, by the way. I've seen you around the cottages. You're staying in the mint green one, aren't you?"

"I am."

"The cottages are really nice, aren't they? They used to be a bit rundown. But I loved them anyway."

"You've come here before?"

A quick look of... something... flashed across Rose's face. "Ah, yes. Every year."

"Back when they were... what were they? Murphy's?"

"Yes, they were Murphy's Resort. But Violet sure has spruced them up. But somehow, they still seem homey and... special."

"They do." She nodded, agreeing with Rose.

"I love coming out here to catch the sunrise. Well, I guess it's really the reflected sunrise since we're facing west. But the colors still are very pretty. Look at that lovely shade of pink beginning to color the clouds." Rose pointed to a tower of clouds with a pale pink blush highlighting its edges.

"It is pretty."

"I come out for the sunsets, too. I do love watching the sky." Rose looked up at the sky, brightening above the water.

"The sunsets have not disappointed me either, that's for sure." She picked up a handful of sand and let it slip through her fingers, enjoying the simple conversation. Moonbeam seemed full of nice people. A slower lifestyle. She liked the pure ease of the flow of life here.

Rose turned to her. "Are you here alone, too?"

Now that was a hard question to answer. "I'm staying alone in the cottage. But... well, my sister is staying in the cottage next to me." She paused, then plunged ahead, uncertain why she was telling this stranger her story. "I just found out she's my sister. It's kind of crazy. My mom gave her up for adoption when she was like three and I thought she was just an imaginary friend."

Rose's forehead crinkled. "An imaginary friend?"

"I guess after she left, I kept talking about her, and eventually Mom convinced me Willow was an imaginary friend."

"But she's real."

"Very real."

"How did you find out about her?"

"Oh, that was one of Magnolia—my mother's—surprises. Set this all up with her estate lawyer. I found out she's gone now. But I haven't seen her since she left when I was seventeen."

"That's a lot to deal with. And how do you feel about all of this?"

How did she feel? Mad. Happy. Uncertain.

"I really don't know. I admit, I'm afraid that after this week… that Willow will go back to her life, and I'll go back to mine. I won't have any family, just like before."

"Is that what you want?" Rose asked quietly.

"No…"

"Have you talked to Willow about what happens next with you two?"

"No."

"Maybe you should. It would be a shame to miss out on…" Rose looked out at the water before continuing. "Miss out on having a sister. Sharing things with her."

Rose was probably right…

"So, where is home for you?" Rose asked.

"I don't really have a home now. I just packed up and left the last place. I'm moving up north by Georgia." It was getting easier to almost believe that was where she was headed. That she had a plan.

"So you have a new job, but you still need to look for an apartment?"

"Yes, I still need to find an apartment." That part was true. Needed to find an affordable place. Not like here in Moonbeam. She'd priced apartments here on a whim... and they were way out of her waitressing budget. Not surprising, since it was a coastal town.

"I'm sure you'll land where you're supposed to land. We always do." Rose gave her an easy, encouraging smile.

She hoped Rose was right.

Willow woke up and rolled over in bed. Derek wasn't there, and his side of the bed was cold. No surprise. He usually got up really early. She could smell the coffee. She slipped out of bed, quickly got dressed, and padded out barefoot into the front room. He was sitting at the table with his laptop open before him.

"Good morning." She walked over and poured a cup of coffee.

"Good morning, sleepyhead."

"Hey, it's only seven." She walked over and

kissed his neck, so glad to have him here with her.

He grinned. "Been up for two hours."

"Of course you have." She shook her head. "You working?"

"I do have to do a few things this morning. Sorry. I left in such a hurry."

"No, that's okay. Do what you need to do."

"Why don't you go knock on Aspen's door and see if she wants to go to breakfast with you? It will give you two more time to talk." Derek suggested.

"That's a good idea." She slipped on a pair of shoes by the door and crossed to Aspen's cottage. She didn't answer the door. Disappointed, she turned to head back to her cottage when she spied Aspen coming up from the beach. Willow waved as Aspen jogged up.

"Morning. I was up watching the sunrise."

"I was wondering if you wanted to catch breakfast? Maybe go to Sea Glass Cafe?"

"Sure, that sounds great. Derek coming?"

"He's got some work to do. I'll bring him back something or he can scrounge through that basket we got."

"Give me five minutes," Aspen said.

She headed back to her cottage and went

inside. Derek was talking on his cell phone. She finished getting ready, gave him a quick kiss on the cheek while he continued his call, and headed out.

Aspen came out of her cottage at the same time. "Walk?" Aspen asked.

"Yes, that sounds good." She didn't really have the time to take walks back home. It was always go, go, go. And always in the car.

They headed out to the street. "You seem to really know your way around town. I'm still getting lost," she said as they crossed a side street and suddenly were on the main street, Magnolia.

"I'm getting the hang of it. I love being in a town where you can walk everywhere."

"Where I live, it's a fifteen, twenty-minute drive to the closest grocery store. Twenty to thirty minutes to Eli's school. Everything is off the interstate. This is kind of a nice change."

They got to Sea Glass Cafe and stepped inside. The delicious aroma of cinnamon and rich coffee swirled around them. A woman called to them from across the room. "Take a seat anywhere. I'll be there in a jiffy."

They sat at a table by the window. The woman walked up with two menus. "Hi. I'm

Melody. Welcome to Sea Glass Cafe. Evelyn— she's one of the owners—made fresh cinnamon rolls today."

"I smell them." Aspen grinned. "I'm going to have to have one of those. And coffee."

"I'll have the same," Willow said without even looking at the menu. She'd normally order a fruit platter, or maybe some yogurt. But today she was going to throw caution to the wind and eat one of those decadent-smelling cinnamon rolls.

"Good choice," Melody said and walked back toward the kitchen.

"This place is so cute," Willow said as she looked around at the delightful beach decorations on the walls and vases full of sea glass and shells.

"It is."

Melody returned with their coffee and cinnamon rolls. The rolls were big and fluffy and smothered with pecans and a caramel glaze. She almost moaned looking at them. How many calories in that thing? But she ignored that thought and took a bite. "Oh my gosh. This is delicious."

Melody smiled. "They really are good, aren't they?"

"We might have to come back every morning of our stay," Aspen said as she took a second bite.

"Where are you two staying?"

"At Blue Heron Cottages."

"Oh, my friend Violet owns them. Aren't they darling?"

"They're really nice." Willow nodded.

"She did such a great job restoring them. She works non-stop with them though. Did you know she has a happy hour for all the guests on Fridays? You should make sure to go to it. Just some appetizers and wine or beer. But it's fun. I try to drop by when I can."

"We'll try to make sure to go to it," Aspen said.

"Let me know if you need anything else. I'll bring out refills for your coffee soon." Melody headed back to the kitchen.

"Everybody knows everything about everyone here in Moonbeam." Willow laughed.

"Small towns. Gotta love 'em." Aspen grinned knowingly.

So had she lived in a small town? "I've never lived in one. Always a big city. How about you?"

"I've lived in quite a few. Though I'm not sure if you really belong if you're not born and raised in the town." Aspen shrugged. "At least in larger towns, there are more people drifting in and out. Easier to blend in."

She glanced over at Aspen. Did she like to get lost in the crowd? Blend in? She really hadn't said much about her past. She'd told Aspen like every little detail of her life, she realized. But Aspen? Not so forthcoming on hers.

"Aspen, you haven't said where you live."

"I... uh... I'm in the middle of moving. Headed up to Georgia." Aspen didn't look up.

"Really?"

"Yeah, it was time for a change."

"That's kind of exciting. You have a new job lined up?"

Aspen nodded. "Sure."

"What do you do?"

"I... I usually work retail or in the restaurant business."

"Oh, managing those is hard work with long hours."

Aspen just nodded again.

"When do the movers get there?"

Aspen stared at her. "Huh?"

"The moving company. When will they get there with your things?"

"Oh… my things. My things will get there next week." Aspen looked down at her cinnamon roll, picking off the pecans with her fork.

"Don't you like pecans?" she asked.

"What?" Aspen looked up in surprise. "Yes, I do. I was saving them for last. My favorite part."

She laughed. "You know, Eli does that. Picks off nuts to eat them last. Or saves the icing on the cake for last. His favorite."

"Sounds like your son is my kind of person." Aspen grinned.

They continued chatting through breakfast, but Willow realized that Aspen had still not told her much about her life. Maybe she was just a private person. She'd hoped that by staying in Moonbeam this week she'd get to know her sister better. But… even though they'd talked a lot, she still didn't feel like she knew Aspen very well.

CHAPTER 12

Aspen showed up a little before four p.m. for her shift at Jimmy's. Walker greeted her as she entered. "Hey you. Thanks so much for helping out. Can you believe we had another server call in sick today? I don't know what's going on. We rarely have people out. Workers stay with us for years. Heck, I think we're a great place to work." He shrugged. "Just a bad couple of weeks here. And we're going to be headed into busy season when all the snowbirds come down."

"Snowbirds?"

"The people who winter here. Moonbeam really fills up with them. It seems like half the town is seasonal residents. Don't mind it though. They keep us busy."

"Well, I'm ready to work. You want me at the hostess station?"

"Yes, that will be great."

"It's kind of slow now. You have something for me to do until it picks up? Roll some napkin rolls, fill the salt shakers? Anything?"

"That would be great. I'll send out some bins of silverware and napkins. Can you work at that table right there? You'll still be able to see if people come in."

"I've got it."

"Have I told you how glad I am that you're in town this week?" He gave her a wide grin, his eyes twinkling. And it made her feel special. And needed. She liked that.

"Glad I could help." She ignored the warm blush on her cheeks at his words.

"And if you don't have plans after work, want to have dinner when the rush is over?"

"I'd like that." Dinner with Walker again. It was getting to be a habit. A habit she enjoyed.

"Great." He smiled again and headed away. Soon a server came out with silverware and napkins and set them out on the table. She sat down and expertly wrapped the napkin rolls. Something she'd done a million times in her life. She could do it without even looking.

So it gave her time to think… which could be good or bad. Walker had asked her to eat with him again. Probably just doing the friendly thing. Only… there was that whole don't-make-friends rule that she was obviously breaking.

But then, she was breaking a lot of her rules this week. Like the never-lie rule. But she hadn't exactly *lied* to Willow today at breakfast. Her things *were* going to be delivered next week, wherever she ended up. They'd just be delivered by the trunk of her car, not a moving company.

She guessed she really did have to go look for a job up in Georgia now that she'd told so many people she was headed that way. And she *would* have a job when she got there… You know, after she found one. So saying she had one wasn't really a full lie. She sighed. She couldn't bear for Willow to know what her life was really like. Not since Willow had such a perfect life. She didn't want her sister to think less of her. Think that she was some kind of failure. She was the big sister, after all. Wasn't Willow supposed to look up to her? But how could she look up to someone who lived out of her car and didn't have a job?

She pushed the thought away and continued rolling the silverware, seating just two couples that came in. She was sure it would pick up soon. She sat back down, thinking about the woman she'd met today on the beach. Rose. She was staying at the last cottage of the resort. The one painted a peach color. The colors Violet had picked out for the cottages really did give the resort a cheerful ambiance.

She and Rose had walked back up from the beach after watching the sunrise. The woman was friendly but had something about her. A sadness, maybe.

Or maybe she'd imagined that. Rose sure was easy to talk to. Some people were just like that.

A group of four people came in, and she jumped up to seat them. Soon it was a constant stream of customers, and she juggled greeting them, seating them, keeping a waitlist, and clearing up tables to help out when she could.

Tara dropped by the hostess station. "I don't know what we did without you. Seriously, could you clone yourself and leave one of you behind when you go next week?"

She laughed. "Not sure that's really possible."

"Our loss." Tara shrugged. "Hey, Walker said you're coming to our barbecue tomorrow.

Man, my folks still make the biggest deal out of birthdays. You'd think we were still little kids. Mark my words… there'll even be balloons."

"I think it sounds like fun. You're lucky to have a big family like that."

"I am. I know." Tara started to walk away. "But make sure you don't tell Walker that. I'd deny it."

She continued to work until finally the crowd died down and Walker came by to get her. "Come on. It's time for dinner. Mom's joining us. I convinced her to get off her feet. She's been waiting tables all night."

She followed him out to a four-top table where Sally was already sitting sipping on white wine. They sat down with her.

"Aspen, I really appreciate your help this week. You've really been a godsend." Sally's face shone with genuine gratitude.

"Glad to help." The now-familiar heat of a blush swept across her cheeks. The Bodines were always handing out compliments, and she wasn't used to them.

"And I hear you're coming to Tara's party. Wonderful. We're doing a crawfish boil, hushpuppies, and lots of side dishes. Oh, and a birthday cake, of course."

"Mom goes all out for parties." Walker leaned in close and whispered in an exaggerated tone. "A bit over the top if you ask me."

Sally rolled her eyes at her son. "Heard that. You never seem to complain when it's your birthday."

"But of course, not." He winked at his mother. "I'm worth it."

"Oh, Walker." Sally shook her head but grinned.

"Tell me what you want for dinner, and I'll put in the order." Walker stood.

"I'll have the Caesar salad with shrimp on it," Sally said.

"Oh, that sounds good. I'll have that, too." Aspen's stomach growled just thinking about it.

"Think I'll have one, too. I'll put in the order." Walker headed to the kitchen.

"So, Walker was telling me about your sister. Isn't that wonderful? To find her after all this time? I mean, it's terrible that you missed out on so much, but I'm glad you found her now."

"It's… different. Strange. Like we should know each other better, yet we don't." She fiddled with the napkin roll on the table. One of the hundred or so she'd rolled tonight.

"You're very lucky to have the chance to get

to know her now. You should try and figure out a way to keep in touch often. Family is very important."

She wouldn't know. She'd never had that. But she could tell that the Bodines had some kind of fairy-tale family. Close. Working together. Joking. Teasing. Big family parties. Something she'd only seen in movies and TV shows. And they had it here in real life. Lucky people.

But really, even if she got to know Willow better, she doubted they'd ever have what the Bodines had. You couldn't just find—have that —after only knowing someone for a few days. And that's all she and Willow had had so far. Who knew when—or maybe even if—she'd see Willow again after this week.

"Yes, I'm not sure how we'll work all that out after this week. She has her own family. A really great husband. A son." From a different world than the one she lived in.

"I don't think you should throw away a chance to make it work. To have a family. Not everyone is given the chance."

Walker slid into the seat beside her. "Is Mom giving you advice? That's what she does. Gives advice on everything to everyone." He teased his mother, but Aspen could see the caring in his eyes.

"I was just saying how lucky she is to have found her sister."

"Hey, I have a sister I could share with her. Tara is pretty high maintenance as sisters go."

"She is not." Sally shook her head. "You two. So competitive. I don't know how I ever raised you to be like that."

"I don't know, Mom. You're just lucky, I guess," Walker teased his mother again.

Such an easy banter between all the Bodines. And it was clear they were close and cared deeply about each other. Just like she'd always imagined a family should be.

They ate their meal, and Sally talked about the history of the restaurant. The early years when they first opened. The struggles they had. Aspen found it all fascinating. From the changes they'd made to the menu over the years, to the same high-top tables along the railing, to the grill in the kitchen they were constantly making repairs to but Sally couldn't bear to give up. Said it made the best food and a new one wouldn't be the same.

When they finished, Sally rose. "I'm going to go find your father. I bet he didn't even eat the sandwich I left on his desk. And Walker, you walk Aspen home."

"Yes, ma'am."

After Sally left, she turned to Walker. "You don't have to do that. I can walk home alone."

"Are you kidding me? After my mom said to walk you home?" He raised his eyebrows in faux shock. "Not a chance. If Mom says to walk you home, I walk you home. Besides, I'm kind of getting used to walking home by way of the cottages."

A smile tugged at the corners of her mouth. "Okay, looks like I have an escort then." And she didn't mind that one bit.

Walker led Aspen out of Jimmy's and down the wharf. She looked up at the lights strung above them, like she did each night, her eyes lighting up like a little kid at Christmas. Then—and he knew she'd do it—she stopped to look in the window of the toy store, this time commenting on a mermaid display the shop owner had placed in the storefront window.

They got to the end of the wharf, and he turned to her. "Want to walk home the beach way? There's an almost full moon tonight. Should be nice and bright."

"Sure, that sounds like fun. I don't think I'd walk it at night alone, but let's do it."

He liked that. That she trusted him enough to take the beach way. They headed to the beach, and the moonlight illuminated the shore and tossed light on the frothy foam of the breaking waves. They walked along the shoreline, talking softly in the magical light.

The moon suddenly plunged behind a cloud and the beach darkened. "Well, that makes it harder. It will just take a moment for our eyes to adjust." He reached out, and she looked at him for a moment before placing her hand in his.

Her warm hand sent a shock of connection through him, and he stared down at their interlaced hands before drawing his gaze up to her face. She stood there staring at him. He swallowed. "Okay, ready to try this again?"

She nodded slowly, saying not a word.

They walked down the beach, their eyes adjusting to the lower light of the filtered moon. Then the clouds swept away, and the moonlight streamed down again. But he still held her hand as they walked, enjoying the warmth. Enjoying the connection.

Aspen was an interesting woman. Energetic. A hard worker. But there was a tentative side to her. Like when she talked about her sister. It was almost like she was afraid to let her sister really get to know her.

Or really let him get to know her for, that matter. She knew way more about him than he knew about her. He wanted to change that. "So tell me more about yourself. Your childhood. Where you grew up."

"There's not much to tell."

More of that tentative, secretive side. "There has to be something. Where did you live? Was it just your mom and you? You know, after Willow was gone?" Was he asking too many questions? But he so wanted to get to know her better.

"It was just Mom and me... and her boyfriend of the month. There was always a boyfriend." She stopped and looked up at him. "We moved around a lot. Mom was... gone a lot."

"She left you alone, you mean?"

"Yeah. That."

"I'm sorry."

"No, I don't want you to feel sorry for me. See, this is why I don't talk about my past. I don't want pity. I'm fine. I turned out fine." Her voice was strong and insistent.

"You're more than fine. You're a strong, independent, beautiful woman."

Her brows creased. "I'm not beautiful. Willow is the pretty daughter. That's why Mom knew she'd easily be adopted. She was so pretty and didn't cause trouble or ask questions like I did. She didn't think that anyone would… want me."

His heart squeezed in his chest, but he picked his words carefully. "Aspen…" He reached out and brushed a lock of hair from her face. "You are beautiful. And kind. And so many other words I can think of. And… I'm sorry that you had such a tough childhood. No child should have to live like that."

She shrugged. "It was no big deal."

"It is a big deal," he said softly. "And you survived it. That's impressive. You surprise me more each day that I get to know you."

And he couldn't believe he'd only known her a handful of days. Because… she'd become important to him. He considered her a friend.

"I just did what I had to do." She downplayed his compliment.

She might minimize what she'd gone

through, but he could hardly imagine it. He'd been surrounded by family. Not only his parents and Tara, but uncles, aunts, and dozens of cousins. He hadn't really thought about how extremely lucky he'd been to have all that. It was just something… just something he had. He should tell his mother how much he appreciated her more often. Though he was sure she knew it. But it wouldn't hurt to say the words.

He squeezed Aspen's hand. "I'm still impressed with you." He could see the blush creep across her cheeks. She blushed easily, it seemed. Or maybe she wasn't used to people complimenting her.

So she'd feel more comfortable, he changed topics to Tara's birthday party. "So, you ready for a Bodine bash tomorrow?"

"It sounds like fun. I'll need to pick up a present for her."

"Oh, shoot. I didn't tell you. We don't do presents at these parties. Well, not since we were little kids. My parents believe in giving back to the community. We started a tradition of doing something for a local charity at the birthday parties. Tomorrow we're collecting canned food for the local food bank."

"Wow, that's a nice thing to do."

"It's not like we're wanting for anything." He shrugged. "So we like to help out others who might need it."

"I'll bring some canned food then."

"Much appreciated." He squeezed her hand. "And I know I said that Tara was high maintenance. But she's not. She's a very giving person. She's not into fancy things or designer clothes. She's really down to earth."

"I think she's... wonderful." Aspen stopped walking. "I don't know why you guys seem to have taken me under your wing... but I do appreciate it. It's fun getting to know all you Bodines."

He laughed. "You have no idea. There will be—let's just say—quite a few more Bodines at the party tomorrow."

Her eyes narrowed. "Just how many are we talking about?"

"Uh... lots," he said noncommittally.

"If it's going to be all family, maybe I shouldn't come. I don't want to intrude."

"The more the merrier. And besides, you heard Mom. She's glad you're coming."

Aspen looked unconvinced.

"Hey, we're a friendly crowd. It will be fun."

The doubt was still there in her eyes. Her

warm, honey-brown eyes, speckled with amber flakes. The eyes that drew him in. Made him want to… He pushed the thought away. "But you're coming, right?"

She nodded slowly. "I'll come."

Great. For a minute there, he thought he'd scared her away. And he didn't want that. He really wanted her to come. He wanted to spend as much time as he could with her for this week she was in town. And maybe… she'd come back to visit again soon.

CHAPTER 13

On Thursday, Aspen slipped out to see the sunrise, and Rose joined her again. They didn't talk much, just enjoyed each other's company as the sky brightened and the birds flew by over the rolling waves. She did mention she was headed to the party at the Bodines' and was nervous about going. Rose told her to relax and just have a good time.

Then she headed into town and bought some canned goods to donate at Tara's party. Now she was back at her cottage, staring at her clothes, feeling like nothing was the right thing to wear.

She heard a knock at the door and went to answer it. "Hi, Willow. Come in."

Willow entered the room, perfectly dressed in white slacks and a navy boatneck top. Which only hammered in the fact that she, herself, had nothing suitable to wear.

"What's the matter? You look kind of upset." Willow asked.

"I'm going to a party at the Bodines'. I was just trying to figure out something to wear. But nothing seems right," she grudgingly admitted.

"Here, let me look." Willow started back toward the bedroom.

"No, that's okay." The last thing she needed was Willow seeing her meager wardrobe.

"I bet we can find something."

"I—I didn't really bring anything appropriate."

"I over-packed. Let's go find something of mine."

She laughed. "Yours won't fit me. You're a good four inches taller than me and I've got to have twenty pounds on you."

"Stay right there. I'll be right back." Willow disappeared out the door and returned a few minutes later.

"Here, try this." She held out a floral cotton dress. "It's loose-fitting. I think it's too short on me anyway. It should be the perfect length on you."

She looked at the pretty dress. Something she would never buy because it wasn't a practical multi-purpose outfit. And she never would have had a place to wear it. But she did now. And it was lovely…

"Go on. Try it on." Willow nodded and pushed the dress into her hands.

She took the dress and went into the bedroom. After taking off her worn shorts and t-shirt, she let the dress slide onto her. She took a quick look in the mirror. It did fit, and she loved it. She hurried out to show Willow.

Willow clapped her hands. "I knew it would fit. You look lovely in it."

"You sure I can borrow this?"

"No, you can't borrow it. It's yours. Like I said, it's too short on me. It looks much better on you." Willow took a step back. "So… how about I do your hair, too? I'm pretty good at it. We could pull it up. It's probably going to be hot this afternoon."

"I…" She shook her head. "Okay, that sounds nice."

"Be right back." Willow disappeared once

again, then returned with a bag bulging with a curling iron and she didn't know what else.

She eyed it all. "What's all that?"

"Come on. Sit down. This will be fun."

She looked at her sister doubtfully.

Twenty minutes later, she stood and looked in the mirror, barely recognizing the woman in the reflection. Her hair was pulled up in a casual knot, with tendrils drifting down to frame her face. With a touch of warm, brown eyeshadow and a sweep of blush on her cheeks, she looked like a different person. Kind of. The same, yet different.

"Oh…" She continued looking in the mirror.

"You look great." Willow grinned. "I'm pretty good at this if I do say so myself."

"You're a magician." She turned to Willow. "Thank you."

"Always wanted a sister to swap clothes with and help get ready for dates."

"Oh, this isn't a date. I'm just going to the party," she assured Willow.

Willow shrugged and tried to hide a smile. "Whatever you say. But Walker likes you. I can tell."

"No, he doesn't. We're just friends." She

frowned and shook her head. "Just friends." You know, the friends she wasn't supposed to make because of her rule.

"If you say so." Willow gave her a half smile. "But after the party, when you get back here, make sure you come over and tell me all about it."

Aspen's heart filled with… something. A feeling of… sisterhood? Willow wanted to hear about her time at the party. Just like a real sister.

They were real sisters, she realized with a start. Just not typical ones. Ones raised together. But they'd found each other now. Genetically, they were sisters. Now… if they could just find a way to truly feel like sisters.

A memory swept through her of singing Willow to sleep, holding her tiny hand through the rails on the crib and patting her back. She'd loved her so when she was just a small baby. She knew that. Remembered that. Felt that.

Willow took a step closer and hugged her. "You look great. Have a wonderful time."

She stood there in Willow's embrace, shocked. Then she slowly raised her arms and hugged her back. "Thank you for all of this," she whispered.

"Hey, what are sisters for?"

What were sisters for? What would they become? But right now, she just enjoyed hugging her sister. And for a brief moment, she felt like she belonged. That she had family.

CHAPTER 14

Violet hurried into Parker's General Store. Donna, the owner, greeted her as she entered. "Hi, Violet."

"Donna, hi. I came in for some more paint. I didn't dare send Rob in to get it. I want to repaint the lobby. It's still just a boring beige color. I'm thinking a light sea green would look nice."

"You know where the paint is." Donna nodded toward the back of the store.

She laughed. "I sure do. I'm pretty sure I single-handedly made your profit for that section of the store."

She went to the paint section and looked over the color charts. She debated between two colors. She headed back to ask Donna's opinion, but she was busy helping other customers. She took the color swatches and headed through the connecting walkway to Sea Glass Cafe. Maybe Melody could help.

She found Melody behind the ice cream counter. "Hey, Melody. I'm buying some paint."

Melody laughed. "So, that's not new."

"Okay, okay. I know I've done a lot of painting. But now I want to do the lobby. I Can't decide between these two colors." She held up the swatches.

Melody's eyebrows furrowed as she stared at the colors. "They are both good, I think. But that one on the left is a bit more of a cool color. That one on the right is warmer."

She stared at the two samples. "I can't decide."

"I don't think you'll go wrong with either one."

She let out a long sigh. "Maybe I'll get a sample of each and go from there."

"That's a good idea." Melody nodded. "You want to stay and have some ice cream?"

"You know? I think I will." She climbed onto the stool. "I'll have vanilla with some of that great chocolate sauce that Evelyn makes."

"Coming right up." Melody dished up the

ice cream, smothered it with chocolate sauce, added a dollop of fresh whipped cream, and slid it across the counter.

She sank her spoon into the delicious-looking feast. "So are you coming to the happy hour tomorrow?"

"I'm going to try."

"Haven't seen you and Ethan there for a while. Why don't you ask him to come, too? Tell him I specifically invited him."

"If I see him."

She hid a smile. Ethan found a reason to come into Sea Glass Cafe almost every day. He obviously had a crush on Melody, but she never seemed to notice. "If you see him, have him come with you."

Melody nodded. "Oh, I met a couple of women staying at Blue Heron Cottages."

"That must have been Aspen and Willow. They're sisters." But she didn't think it was her place to tell the whole story about how they'd just found out.

"They said they love the cottages."

That was always nice to hear. "Glad they do." She loved running the resort. She just wished she was booked up with more guests. Though next week she had people coming in for a wedding next weekend at the resort. That was nice. The wedding party was staying at the cottages and having the wedding in the courtyard. A nice boost of income for off-season.

As if on cue, Ethan came walking up to the ice cream counter. "Hi, Ethan. We were just talking about you."

"You were?" He smiled shyly at Melody and slipped onto a stool.

"I was saying that you and Melody should come to happy hour at the cottages tomorrow."

"I could do that." He looked expectantly at Melody. "Do you want to go?"

"I think I could get away."

"I could come by here and we could walk over together," Ethan suggested, his expression hopeful.

"That sounds nice."

Ah, her work here was done. She stood up. "I should go get my paint samples. I'll see you both tomorrow then." She walked back to the general store, smiling. That was almost Ethan asking Melody out…

She got her samples and went back to the cottages. Rob's car was gone, which was good. Maybe she could paint both samples before he got back and rolled his eyes at her. Why she'd thought that this boring beige was a good color for the lobby was beyond her. It had covered up the dingy white walls that had been here, but the color she thought would be a light "paper bag" beige just looked… dull.

She found the paintbrushes and painted the samples out on two different walls in big splashes of color. Then she stood in the middle of the room staring at them, still undecided.

The door opened and Rose came into the lobby. "Hello, Rose."

Rose looked at the colors painted on the walls. "You trying to decide which one?"

"I am."

Rose pointed to the cooler shade of sea green, just a touch greener than the other shade. "That one."

She looked at the paint patches again. Rose was right. "Thank you. I was having the hardest time deciding. I agree with you. That color is best. I want to brighten up the lobby a bit."

"I think that color will do that for you."

"Now, was there something I can do for you?" She turned from staring at the splotches of paint.

"I was wondering… I know this is last

minute. But I was wondering if I could stay in my cottage for a while longer. Maybe two more weeks? Or are you all filled up?"

"No, you can stay. That would be fine." She'd planned to put some people from next week's wedding in the peach cottage, but she could move them to the blue cottage. That would work.

Rose's face lit up, though she'd swear it still didn't reach her eyes. There was something mysterious about her. "That's great. I thought I'd treat myself to a bit longer stay."

She hadn't completely booked the resort any week through the rest of the year, though she was hoping come January when everyone was escaping the cold up north that she'd fill up. As far as she was concerned, Rose was welcome to stay as long as she liked.

"I was thinking of running to Parker's to pick up the paint I chose. There's no one checking in. But I'm always worried that someone might drop by and ask for a room. I really hate putting up the be-back-soon sign."

"You're only one person. You should get some help. You can't do everything."

She laughed. "You sound just like Robbie.

But I do need to get some part-time help. I should start looking."

"You should. Good luck with your painting," Rose said as she turned and walked out of the lobby.

She turned and stared at the walls again. Rose was right. Robbie was right, as much as she hated to admit that—and she wouldn't actually *tell* him he was right. She did need to get help.

And she couldn't wait to paint this lobby and get rid of the boring beige.

CHAPTER 15

Aspen stood in front of the Bodines' house debating turning around and going back to the cottages. Laughter and music drifted from the backyard. She hadn't been expecting a house like this. A large, two-story house with a welcoming porch that stretched all across the front of it with a crisply painted white railing.

A really large house. With a round alcove jutting out on the far side of the upper floor. And she was fairly certain that was what they called a widow's walk up on the rooftop. The house sat directly on the harbor. She had no idea that Walker came from a family who could afford a home like this. A *mansion* like this.

Even with Willow's pretty dress and her

fancy hairstyle, she knew that she wasn't going to fit in here. She spun on her heels and turned to head back to her cottage.

"Aspen, there you are. Glad you made it." Walker came walking through the gate to the backyard dressed in nice khaki shorts and a collared, knit, short-sleeve shirt in a light blue color.

He looked smashingly handsome. Not that she noticed, because he was just a friend. No, not a friend. She didn't make friends. She sighed. Only… the Bodines had become friends, no matter how many times she repeated her rule to herself.

Too late to leave now. She gave him a weak smile. "I made it."

"Come on back. I'll introduce you to everyone. But don't think you have to remember names because… well, we have a yard full."

He took her elbow and led her to the backyard. She gasped at the view stretched out before her. The house was situated on a small hill, and the expanse of the harbor rolled out from the shore. The sun sparkled off the bay while a large boat cut through the water, leaving a trail of wake behind it. "Wow." The only word she could manage to say.

"Yeah, it's great, isn't it? Never gets old. I can't tell you how many hours of my life I've spent out here just staring at the bay or fishing off the dock."

"Lucky man." She turned and set her bag of canned goods on a table piled high with bags of food, still impressed with the giving attitude of the Bodines.

"Come on. Let me introduce you around."

Within fifteen minutes, she was certain she'd met a hundred people. Just how large a family did Walker have?

Tara walked up to her. Thank goodness. A familiar face. "Tara, happy birthday."

"Thank you." Tara gave her a quick hug, then tilted her head toward a large table spread with trays of crawfish and hushpuppies. "See, I told you. And see the balloon centerpiece?" Tara rolled her eyes. "Mom just can't resist. I swear she thinks I'm still five."

She thought it all looked wonderful. Large tables were spread around for people to eat at. Festive music played just loud enough to be heard, but easy to talk over. She'd never had a birthday party in her entire life, and this one enchanted her. "I think it's wonderful."

Sally walked over to them. "Aspen, so nice

of you to come. I'd love for you to meet my sisters. Come with me."

Walker leaned in close and whispered in her ear. "Just so you know, she has four sisters…"

She swallowed hard as she followed Sally across the yard, missing the comfort and familiarity of Walker at her side. She tossed a glance back toward him but he was deep in a conversation with his cousin? Second cousin? Something like that. She was sure she'd met him. Hadn't she?

Walker kept an eye on Aspen as she met all his mother's sisters. And more. She looked a bit overwhelmed. He should probably go rescue her. He stepped away from the group of six cousins who had gathered under the live oak and crossed over to Aspen.

He stopped next to his mother. "Hey, Mom. Great party as usual. You throw the best parties."

She eyed him. "Why the compliment? Are you in trouble?"

He laughed and kissed her cheek. "Nah, just

wanted to tell you that you're the best Mom, ever."

"You sure you didn't get into trouble?"

"Cross my heart." He brushed his fingers in a cross over his chest.

His mother shot him a doubtful look but turned back to her sisters. He leaned close to Aspen. "Hey, you want to go down near the water? Take a break from meeting people?"

"Yes. That would be great." Her words came out in a rush, and he laughed.

He led her down to the water's edge, then stepped down to the dock along the sea wall. They sat on a bench, and Aspen looked a bit dazed.

"You doing okay?"

She gave a little laugh. "I am. But you sure have a big family."

"Hey, some of those folks are friends. Well, a few of them." He winked at her. "You're doing great."

"I don't know. I still don't have your mom's sisters' names figured out."

"You mean Susan, Silvia, Samantha, and Savannah? You'd think my grandmother would have run out of S names, wouldn't you?" He laughed. "And her brother—he's out of town this week—his name is Steve."

"How in the world did your grandmother keep them all straight?"

"No clue." He shrugged. "But Mom didn't follow the S tradition, obviously."

"Your family is… huge." Aspen looked up at him, her eyes wide. "How do you even remember everyone's name?"

"Grew up with all of them. You should see the holidays. They are crazy. We rotate going to different houses on Thanksgiving and Christmas. This is our year for Christmas. We're closing down Jimmy's and having the family there. Giving the employees the day off. The family will help serve up a big meal."

"You don't get presents for this family, do you?" She eyed him.

"Nah, just my folks and Tara. The extended family is doing a toy drive this year at the restaurant. Customers will drop off toys in a big barrel we'll have at the hostess station. Then, the family will get together about a week before Christmas and wrap them all. We coordinate with a few churches in the area to distribute the toys to families that can use the help."

"You guys are really into this giving thing, aren't you?"

"My grandmother always said that the Bodines have been blessed, and we should spread our blessings around. So we do." It was as simple as that. They'd all been raised to give back.

"Well, it's impressive. Very nice of your family."

Suddenly it was he who was uncomfortable with the compliments. He changed the subject. "So, you recovered from the people? We could go up and eat."

"I've never had crawfish before. I'm kind of looking forward to it."

"You're in for a treat. Come on. I'll show you how it's done." He got up and reached down a hand for her and pulled her to her feet. Then he kept her hand in his as they walked back up to the food. Her hand felt... *right*... securely ensconced in his.

Aspen mastered the art of eating crawfish. They were delicious and messy, and she enjoyed every bite. She pushed back from the tray of food between Walker and her. "I can't eat another bite."

He pushed back, too. "I'm kind of full myself."

The party still was going in full force. A few couples were dancing out in a gazebo at the edge of the yard. It was like the whole yard was made to have parties in it. Everyone in his family had been so friendly and welcoming. She couldn't even imagine what it was like belonging to a large family like this.

If she was lucky, she and Willow would keep in touch. She wasn't certain if that would happen or not. Though she should really take Rose's advice and talk to Willow. See if they could arrange to meet up again. Keep in touch. But she had to admit, she was afraid of being rejected. That Willow, even if she had good intentions of keeping in touch, would be too busy with her own life.

"Whatcha thinking?" Walker leaned forward.

"I... nothing much. Just how nice it must be to have a family like this. All the things you do together."

"It is nice. It was fun growing up with so many cousins. Now my cousins are having kids and all those kids will grow up together."

"Doesn't anyone ever move away?"

"A few do. Most come back, though. They live in Moonbeam, or over on Belle Island, or a few live in Sarasota. You know, crazy people who want big city life."

She wouldn't consider Sarasota a *big* city. A fair-sized town, yes. But big? But she figured it was all relative. Most any city was way larger than Moonbeam. "Belle Island. That's near here?"

"It is. Just the other side of the bay. Pretty place with great beaches. And I hate to admit it, but some wonderful places to eat. Like Magic Cafe. It's owned by a wonderful woman, Tally. Really great food. I'm glad she's over on Belle Island instead of here in Moonbeam. She'd give Jimmy's a run for their money." His mouth curved into a relaxed grin. "Too bad you're not staying longer. I'd take you over so you could try it."

That did sound like fun, but she was leaving in two days. Not a lot of time to explore. And tomorrow was another meeting with the lawyer.

"What was that thought? You just frowned," Walker cocked his eyebrow.

He did that. Picked up on little things. She wasn't sure if she liked it or if it threw her off a bit. For sure, she wasn't used to anyone paying that much attention to her. "Oh, I was thinking about tomorrow morning. Willow and I have another meeting with the lawyer. No idea what he's going to say this time. I think that Magnolia is about finished with her surprises, but then why does he want to see us again? Maybe some paperwork on her estate or something."

"Probably. You'll have to let me know what he says." He gave her a supportive smile. He was always supportive. Easy to talk to.

She was going to miss him...

She stared at him for a moment, and before she knew what she was doing, the words just blurted out. "Any chance you can come to happy hour at the cottages tomorrow? We could talk then. But I know it's a Friday. You're probably busy at Jimmy's."

"Just so happens I'm off tomorrow night. I'd love to come. I'll drop by your cottage about five?"

"Sure. Sounds great." Now she knew that

she'd at least see him tomorrow. Maybe for the last time before she left Moonbeam. A twinge settled deep inside her that she totally ignored.

Jimmy walked up to them. "Son, I hate to ask this. But the cook just called. There's a mess up on the order that came in this afternoon. He's low on items he needs for tonight. Think you could run over and deal with it? I would, but your mother insisted that I stay here at the party."

"Sure thing, Dad. I'll go right over." Walker stood and appeared to not mind at all to be send back to the restaurant.

She got up, too. "I should probably head out, too. I'm supposed to meet up with Willow." And she didn't think she could face all these people without Walker being here, even if they were all nice and welcoming.

"You don't have to leave," Walker insisted.

"I really need to meet up with Willow."

"Okay then. I'm going to drive to Jimmy's. Can I give you a ride?"

As tempting as it was, she'd just walk. She needed time to walk off the meal and time to think. "Thanks for the offer, but I think I'll just walk."

"You sure?"

She nodded.

"Okay, I've got to run." He headed out through the gate, and she suddenly felt alone in the mass of people.

She headed over to thank Sally for having her, then slipped out the gate and headed down the road toward Blue Heron Cottages. The afternoon had warmed up quite a bit without much of a breeze. The heat of the sun flushed her cheeks, and she was beginning to regret turning down the ride.

She finally made it back to the Blue Heron, went into her cottage, and kicked off her shoes, throwing herself across the bed. So, that's how some people lived who had big families. And money. They had to have money to afford a big house like that on the harbor. It was all so foreign to her.

She wondered if Derek and Willow had a big family like that. Maybe Willow had aunts and uncles and cousins in her adopted family. She'd never asked her that. Maybe there would be no room in all that for her. And even if she did visit, would she feel like an outsider like she had today at the Bodines', no matter how hard everyone tried to make her feel welcome?

She ached, deep inside, to be part of a family like that. But that would never be her reality. It wasn't hers to have. Fate had been stingy to her in the family department.

CHAPTER 16

"**A**spen came back from her party." Derek turned from the window to face Willow.

She put down the magazine she'd been leafing through, *Beach Life*. A magazine full of coastal decorating and scrumptious recipes. "Oh, I can't wait to talk to her. I think I'll run over to her cottage."

"That's fine. I need to check my email. Ask her if she wants to go to dinner with us at that Sea Glass Cafe you said was so good."

"I knew you saw their sign when we were walking downtown today. Meatloaf is their special tonight."

"Really?" He gave her a lazy grin and held out his hands in surrender. "What can I say? I might have seen that. And meatloaf is my comfort food."

"I'm well aware of that." She tried dozens of meatloaf recipes after they got married, trying to find the perfect one. She'd found one that he really loved, though he'd said he loved all of them.

She rose from the sofa and brushed a kiss on his cheek. "I'll be back soon."

She crossed to Aspen's cottage and knocked. Soon, the door swung open. "Willow, hi. I was just going to pour some ice tea that I made earlier today. Want some?"

"I do."

"Come in."

She stepped inside and waited while Aspen poured the drinks. "Are you going to tell me all about your date... I mean, about the *party*?"

They went outside and sat on the porch. The ceiling fan made lazy circles above them. Aspen fanned her face with a magazine. "Got a little warm walking home."

"It is a humid one today." She took a sip of her tea. "Now, about the party?"

"It was fine."

"Fine? That's all I'm going to get?"

"Okay, okay. For starters, I think he has like a thousand people in his family. Aunts—his mom has four sisters. And uncles and cousins. I met so many people. And I had crawfish for the first time. Really good, but oh so messy."

"Messy but wonderful, isn't it? And you and Walker had a good time?"

"We did. He's a nice man."

"Good looking, too." She watched Aspen's face, sure she was seeing a spark of interest in her eyes. "You like him, don't you?"

"No, it's not like that."

"I think it is," she insisted, watching the two spots of pink gathering on her sister's cheeks.

Aspen let out a long sigh. "Okay, I admit it. He's a great guy. I really enjoy spending time with him. But we're leaving Saturday. What's the point?"

"The point is, you like him. He likes you. I can tell by the way he looks at you."

"I've only known him a few days." Aspen shook her head slowly. "I don't believe in any of that love at first sight stuff."

She raised her eyebrows. "Sometimes that's all it takes. I swear I fell in love with Derek the first time I met him. And look at us now."

179

"Really? From first sight?"

"Yes. From first sight. I don't know how, but I just knew he was the one for me."

"But I don't really know how I feel about Walker, though. He's fun and attentive and we laugh a lot when we're together. I could talk to him for hours on end."

She wondered if Walker had found out more than she had about Aspen's past in all their talking. Maybe she'd opened up to him. Maybe.

Aspen set her drink down on the table beside them. "I did ask him to come to happy hour here at the cottages tomorrow."

"Well, that's progress."

"I guess. I can't believe I asked him. But still. I want to spend more time with him before we leave." Aspen's eyes sparkled in anticipation.

"You could come back and visit him again. Or he could visit you in Georgia."

"I don't know. That all gets complicated."

"Sometimes life gets complicated."

Aspen laughed softly. "You mean like when you all of a sudden find out you were given up for adoption as a child and you have a sister you never knew about?"

Willow couldn't control the spontaneous

burst of laughter. "Yes, like that. But I'm glad we found each other." She paused, turning serious. "And I hope we can stay in touch. See each other. I don't want to lose you, now that I've found you." She only hoped that Aspen would let her in. Tell her more about herself and her life.

Aspen swallowed hard, her heart racing uncontrollably at her sister's words. "So, you want to stay in touch after this?"

"Of course. We've been given a rare gift. A sister. I always wanted siblings, and now I have you." Willow's face broke into a contented smile.

"But you already have a big family."

"Derek's family. And it's a big one. Though they do treat me like family ever since we got married, and I adore all of them. But we have room for more. They'll accept you, just like they accepted me." Willow bobbed her head. "I know they will."

But would she ever feel like she belonged? Now that was the question.

"You are planning on staying in touch, right?" Willow's eyes narrowed. "Aspen?"

Here she thought that Willow would just be walking away after this week. Maybe they'd send Christmas cards. Though she moved so often, Willow would probably have a hard time tracking her down.

Then there was the possibility that if she got closer to Willow, her sister would find out the truth about her.

The truth about how she lived. The fact she had no job, no home. That she was basically living out of her car. No, she didn't want her to find that out. She didn't want *anyone* to find out. It was her own embarrassing secret to keep.

But here Willow was. Wanting to stay connected. Stay in touch. Her heart squeezed in her chest, knowing that she was taking a chance. That Willow could easily disappear from her life just like Magnolia had. She took a deep breath, taking a risk, hoping she was making the right decision and it wouldn't backfire on her. "I... I'd like to stay in touch. See you when we can work it out. I know you're busy."

Willow reached out and took her hand. "Aspen, I'll never be too busy for you. Never."

And the tiny hope began to grow inside her that maybe, just maybe, she and Willow could really become a family.

Only, if that happened, Willow might find out all her secrets...

CHAPTER 17

Aspen's heart lifted the next morning when she saw Rose sitting on the beach, waiting for sunrise. She hurried over and plopped down beside her. "Good morning."

"Morning, Aspen." Rose smiled at her. "How was your party?"

"It was actually really fun. Lots of people. The Bodines have a huge family. They're all nice, though."

"I'm glad you had a good time. And that young man who invited you. Walker, was it? Did you have a good time with him?"

"He's nice. I even invited him to happy hour here tonight."

"Oh, good. I'll get to meet him." Rose's eyes sparkled.

"He has become a friend. But that's all. Just a friend. I mean, I'm leaving tomorrow, so it can't be more than that."

"Can't it?" Rose tilted her head. "It could be if you wanted it to. There's always a way. A very long time ago I made an impossible relationship work."

"But we just met."

"Sometimes our heart knows how we feel before our brain does."

"I don't know how I feel," she insisted. "Not in my heart or my brain."

"Like I said, sometimes our heart knows if we just listen to it."

Maybe Rose was right, but Aspen couldn't really convince herself that what she felt for Walker was real. Not this quickly. And how did she really feel, anyway? It was all so confusing. This whole week had been so bewildering. Really, driving to a new town and finding a new job sounded easier than this week had been.

Though she had to admit, her heart raced when she saw Walker. That momentary surge of happiness when she first saw him each day. It was so unexpected.

So much unexpected this week…

Rose leaned back on her elbows and

stretched her legs out. "I saw you and Willow out talking on the porch yesterday. Did you sort things out with her?"

Aspen nodded. "She says that she wants to keep in touch." If only it really did work out like that. She wasn't convinced that she wouldn't get lost in the shuffle when Willow went back to her real life. But at least Willow had said they should try to stay in touch.

"That's wonderful. A sister can be a really important part of your life."

"Do you have a sister?"

Rose looked out at the water. "I did. I mean I do. I just don't see her anymore." She shrugged. "These things sometimes happen. Families can be complicated. But you should grab at your chance to stay close to Willow. It's a gift you've been given and you shouldn't waste it."

"I hope we can stay close. We'll see."

They stopped talking while the sky burst into shades of pink and touches of peach. Even the waves quieted down in deference to the brilliant display above them. Finally, the pinks receded, and the sky brightened into a stunning shade of azure.

Rose sighed. "That was lovely, wasn't it?"

"It was," she agreed as she got to her feet.

Rose sprang up beside her, amazingly agile for her age.

Come to think of it, she really had no idea what age Rose was. Older. Much older. But still young in some ways. But she had an older-wiser aura about her.

Rose brushed some sand off her slacks. "I'll miss sitting out here with you in the morning. I talked to Violet and I'm going to stay for another few weeks."

"You are? That sounds so nice."

"Any chance you could stay another week?"

"Ah, no. No chance." She couldn't even afford another *night* after this paid-for week was over.

They headed back toward the cottages, arm in arm. She'd miss these mornings with Rose, too.

"Are you ready for this?" Aspen asked Willow as they stood on her front porch, ready to head into town. She shifted nervously from foot to foot, uncertain what the day had in store for them.

"I guess so. I'm not sure what else he could say after the bomb he dropped last time." Willow tipped her face to the sun as they stepped off the porch. The sun's rays turned her hair into golden threads.

Willow was so beautiful. She was dressed impeccably as usual. A pair of slacks with a precise crease. A blue blouse that made her sky-blue eyes shine. Once again, it was patently clear to her that she paled in comparison to her sister. But she shoved the thoughts away. "You're right. After her last announcement, who knows. But Mr. Brown sounded insistent that we meet again."

They headed into town, walking slowly along the sidewalks. Aspen was in no hurry to get to Brown and Bates. She was a bit afraid of what Magnolia had in store for them this time. Not to mention, she was enjoying this time with Willow. Soon all this would be over. They'd go back to their separate lives. Willow looked over at her and smiled.

She was going to miss this. This time with her sister. What a crazy week it had been. And the fact they were leaving tomorrow was like a sign over her head, following her around, reminding her. She pushed the thoughts away and concentrated on Willow telling her a story of Eli's antics.

Soon they were seated in the conference room at the law firm, and Mr. Brown bustled in and sat at the end of the table. "Ladies, nice to see you again." He sat down and shuffled some files he set on the table.

She squirmed in her chair. Just get on with it, Mr. Fancy Pants lawyer. She glanced over at Willow who sat next to her with a carefully masked face, devoid of emotion. If only she could pull that off too.

"So, I hope you two had a pleasant week." Mr. Brown nodded at them but didn't really seem to expect much of an answer. More of an awkward way to get into whatever he needed to discuss.

"It was lovely," Willow said, her face still neutral.

"Yes, lovely," she echoed, although her words sounded empty.

"Well, good, good. Now, to get on to the matter at hand."

She swallowed and gripped the armrest on her chair. A steel armrest, covered in a leather pad that stuck to her arms, annoying her. Each second dragged on, seeming like an eternity.

Tiiiick, tooooock. Yes, let's get to the matter at hand.

"I have another letter from Magnolia." He efficiently straightened the papers in front of him.

She swallowed a sigh. Of course he did. What now?

"Would you like me to read it to you both?"

She glanced over at Willow, who nodded. She looked at Mr. Brown-of-the-unexpected-news. Could he outdo himself this time? Or, more accurately, could Magnolia outdo herself? "Yes, that would be fine," she said with false agreeableness.

He slowly opened the letter, set it on the table, and smoothed out the creases. Really? How long did it take to get it ready to read? She wanted to reach over and grab it from him but instead just gripped the armrest tighter.

He slowly read the letter, emphasizing each sentence.

Dear Girls,

I hope you two have gotten to know each other. You were so close when you were little girls. I'm sorry for splitting you up. For giving you away, Willow, and for being a terrible mother to you, Aspen. I hope both of you can find it in your hearts to forgive me someday.

By now, my lawyer should have been able to locate your father. Mr. Brown is to give you the info today. You can look for your father or not. It's up to you. It wasn't his fault that you never got to know him. I know I said he left us, but I left him. He just didn't make me happy.

Astonishment surged through her at this new revelation. Her mouth dropped open, but there were no words. She snapped her mouth shut as anger jolted through her. Her father hadn't left her? Magnolia had left *him*? It didn't make any sense. Magnolia had always talked about if your father hadn't left then we could have a nicer apartment, or could go out to fancy restaurants, or wouldn't have to move all the time. Magnolia had always blamed it on her father.

Lovely. Just another lie. The woman couldn't tell the truth if her life depended on it. And then she realized the absurdity of the thought. Her mother's life didn't depend on anything now. It was over. Magnolia was gone. And yet… she was so angry at her. This dead woman. This woman who had told so many lies.

Mr. Brown continued, oblivious to the war raging inside her.

Please don't hate me for what I did. I tried my best. I really did. I hope you two both have wonderful lives and are very happy.
Magnolia

Once again, no love, Magnolia. No love, Mom. Just another bombshell.

Mr. Brown cleared his throat. "Ah, but there is a small problem."

What now? She stared at him, holding her breath, not sure she could take another shock.

"I was unable to locate your father. Magnolia didn't give me much to work with. Didn't have any records with his social security number. It's been… difficult."

"So you don't know where he is?" Suddenly she wanted desperately to find her father. Memories of him skittered through her mind. A long walk to the park, holding his hand. Pushing her on the swing. Sitting beside her on the floor by a Christmas tree while she opened a present. Those memories were real. They did happen.

And her father hadn't left her.

"No, I haven't found him." Mr. Brown shook his head. "Obviously your mother thought I would by the time you got this last letter. I'll keep looking for him and will notify you if I find him. Here's a copy of all the information I have." He slid a folder over toward them.

Magnolia never ceased to surprise her. And not in a good way. How could she have just up and left her husband? Or given away her child, for that matter? Aspen's anger threatened to strangle her.

"And there's more."

She closed her eyes. What now? Willow's hand covered hers and she grasped it, looking for a lifeline.

"She left her estate to both of you, but there's an issue."

Aspen had to hold back a laugh. Her mother never had more than fifty dollars to her name. Some estate.

"She married well on her fourth husband."

"Fourth?" The word slipped out in spite of her best intentions. Magnolia had married three more times?

"But his children are contesting the will.

And there's the small problem that I can't locate any divorce filings from Magnolia and your father. Her fourth husband's children have discovered this and are using it to contest the will."

"I don't need anything from her." Once again, the words just slipped out.

"Nevertheless, those are her wishes. I'm hoping to get this all sorted out soon."

"How much is this estate?" She narrowed her eyes.

"It's fairly significant."

"How significant?"

"In the millions."

She choked. "The millions?"

"Yes, so you can see why I'm trying so hard to make sure you get what is due you."

"I'm sure his children think they have some claim to his estate. That only seems reasonable," Willow said.

"He was... ah... a bit older than Magnolia. They are saying she took advantage of him."

Aspen had no doubt that she did. Typical Magnolia. Always looking for an angle. "So, is that it?" She didn't think she could take one more Magnolia surprise.

"For now. I'll keep in touch. Hopefully I'll be able to get her estate settled soon."

"I'm actually more interested in finding my father." She rose. "Willow, you ready to go?"

Willow stood and thanked Mr. Brown graciously. Of course she did. Her sister was polite. Always. Had obviously been raised by someone who taught her good manners.

"Ah, thanks," Aspen added quickly, noticing the insincerity in her voice.

They headed outside, and she took a long, drawn-out breath, sucking in the heavy, salty air. But it did little to clear her thoughts. Settle her nerves.

"Do you think he'll find our father?" Willow asked. "I would love a chance to get to know him."

"He was... great. I don't have that many memories, but what I do have are good ones. He was more attentive than Magnolia. I can't believe she just left him. I remember being so crushed when he left. I couldn't understand it. And all those years she insisted he left us. But then, she was an expert at sneaking away in the middle of the night. And at rewriting the narrative so she looked pretty."

"I think I'll see if Derek knows anyone who

could take this information Mr. Brown gave us and find Father."

"That would be great." Because she had no clue how to track him down. And she desperately wanted to do just that. Find him. Tell him how sorry she was that Magnolia had taken her away from him. That she hadn't known Magnolia had done that. He must have been devastated, shocked that they had just slipped away into the night.

And how could Magnolia have asked in her letter for forgiveness? Was she crazy? That was never going to happen. Never. At least *she* wouldn't forgive her. If Willow did, that was her own decision to make.

Willow's forehead creased. "Do you think Magnolia tricked her husband out of his money? That his children should really inherit it?"

"I wouldn't doubt it. It sounds like classic Magnolia."

"I don't want any money that isn't really ours."

She nodded her head. "I don't want anything from Magnolia. Nothing. As far as I'm concerned, his children can have the estate. I don't want blood money. Not if she tricked some poor old man out of his life's savings."

"I feel the same way."

So they were in agreement. Good. "Hey, let's go to Sea Glass Cafe and grab some lunch. How about that?" Suddenly she was hungry. And wanted to put all of this behind her. Well, not the getting to know Willow part and not the part about finding out her father hadn't left her. She didn't want to put that behind her. She desperately wanted to find him.

But she'd like to put everything involving Magnolia far behind her. And she hoped that someday she'd find a way to deal with this anger raging inside her.

CHAPTER 18

Melody looked up as more customers walked into Sea Glass Cafe. It was those sisters she'd met. What were their names? Trees... Oh, Aspen and Willow. She waved to them and called out. "Take a seat anywhere. I'll be right over."

She finished making a shake for Delbert Hamilton. He might be this fancy businessman who owned Cabot Hotel, but he sure loved his ice cream. "Here you go, Mr. Hamilton."

"Thanks, Melody. I've been out of town for a few weeks. Been missing this. Always the first thing I do when I get back to town. Head here for some ice cream."

"Enjoy." She slipped out from behind the

counter and over to the two sisters. "Welcome back."

"Hi, Melody." The tall blonde one said. Willow, right? Did she have the names right?

She handed them menus. "Do you know what you want to drink?"

"I'm going to have a vanilla shake," Aspen said as she reached for the menu.

"Just water for me," Willow said.

Aspen eyed her. "Really?"

Willow laughed. "Okay, okay. I'll have a vanilla shake, too."

"Two shakes coming up."

When she returned with the shakes, Aspen looked up from her menu. "What do you suggest today? Everything looks wonderful."

"Evelyn made the best roasted chicken today. She has chicken sandwiches on fresh sourdough."

"Sold. I'll have that. With a side of fries." Aspen handed her the menu.

"I'll have the Caesar salad with some of the chicken on top."

She took Willow's menu. "Okay, it won't be long."

She went to the kitchen and turned in the order, then back out to the ice cream counter to check on Mr. Hamilton. "Need anything else?"

"No, I'm fine." He slipped his long spoon back into the malt glass and took another bite. She smiled, watching him relish his shake.

Ethan came walking up to the counter. How had she missed him coming into the cafe? "Hey, Ethan."

He dipped his chin slightly. "Hi, Melody."

"Did you come in for ice cream?"

"Ah… no… I was just passing by. I wanted to check to see if we're still on for tonight?"

"On for tonight?" She frowned. She was missing something here…

"We talked about going to Violet's happy hour." Ethan shifted his stance, hands shoved into his pockets.

"Oh, that's right." She'd forgotten about that.

"You still want to go?" He looked at her, then quickly down at the floor.

"Yes, that sounds fine. Olivia and Emily are working the dinner shift. Oh, and Blake. It should be fine to leave."

"I could stop by here about a quarter 'til five and we could walk over?"

"Yes, that will work."

A large smile spread across Ethan's face. He must really like going to Violet's happy hour. And maybe he just didn't like to go alone. This would work out nicely. Violet had been badgering her to come to another one at the cottages, but she'd been so busy.

"Okay, I'll see you just before five." Ethan turned to leave, and if she wasn't mistaken, he was whistling under his breath.

Nice guy. He sure must not like cooking, though, because he came in regularly for his meals.

"Order up," Evelyn called from the kitchen.

She hurried to grab the sisters' meals. She bet they would love Evelyn's roasted chicken. Everyone did. And maybe she'd tell them about the peach pie. A perfect ending for a good meal.

Aspen decided to drop by Jimmy's after lunch at Sea Glass Cafe. She wanted to tell Walker all about the meeting with the lawyer. She pushed away any analyzing of *why* he was the one she wanted to talk to.

Pretty much pushed it away.

Why was he the first person she thought of when she wanted to talk about what happened?

But he was. He always listened and understood.

Tara greeted her at the hostess station. "Aspen, did you come for a late lunch?"

She laughed. "No, I'm sorry to admit I had lunch with Willow at one of your competitors."

Tara let out an exaggerated sigh. "Ah, it happens. Sad, but it happens."

"I just came to see if I could talk to Walker."

"I think he's back in the office. Go on back."

She headed to the office and paused in the doorway, looking at him sitting at the desk, his head bent, poring over papers spread before him. He looked up and gave her a smile that sent her pulse racing.

"Aspen."

The single word made her heart pound.

He got up and walked around from behind his desk and rested against the front of it. "So, what's up? You got news from the lawyer?"

"I did. And it's a whopper."

"Well, tell me. Don't leave me in suspense." He waggled a finger at her.

"So… we found out our father is alive. And… get this… he didn't leave us. Magnolia snuck out in the middle of the night and left *him*."

"Oh, wow." His eyes narrowed. "You okay?"

"No, I'm not really. I'm so angry at Magnolia. And my poor dad. To come home one day and his family is gone. How could she do that to him? To me?"

"I don't know." His eyes were bright with sympathy.

"All these years I couldn't figure out why he left. I adored him. I thought we had so much fun together. I have these random memories of times with him. And as a kid, I thought it was my fault he left."

"But it wasn't." He reached out and took her hand, squeezing it gently.

"No, it was Magnolia being her crazy self. Wanting what Magnolia wanted. Not what was good for anyone else."

"I'm sorry."

She didn't really want sympathy. She wanted to vent her anger. She shook her head. "Don't be. It just is what it is. But the lawyer is trying to find him. Though Magnolia didn't have much to go on. Willow is going to have Derek see if he can find an investigator who might be able to locate him."

"It's been kind of a rough week for you, hasn't it?"

"It sure has been. I'm ready to get back to normal. Simple. No surprises."

A look flashed over Walker's face, but she couldn't quite pinpoint what it was. Before she could figure it out, Walker's mom poked her head in the door. "Oh, hi, Aspen. I didn't know you were here."

"I just stopped in for a moment."

"Well, it's good to see you. And if I don't see you again before you leave, I just want to say how nice it was for you to jump in and help us this week. We really appreciate it."

"It was nothing."

Sally gave her a quick hug. "If you're ever back in town, make sure you come visit."

"I will."

Sally turned to Walker. "A load of supplies just came in. Your father is wrestling with all the boxes. You think you could go help him? I swear, he thinks he's still sixteen years old."

"Sure thing." Walker pushed off the desk as Sally left.

"I should go," she said, not wanting to be in his way.

"I'll see you tonight at Violet's happy hour, right?"

"Yes, I'll see you then."

She left Jimmy's feeling like there was a mountain of unfinished business between them. Things to be said. But it would have to wait until tonight.

Tonight. Her last night to spend with Walker Bodine. Sadness swept through her. She'd miss all of the Bodines. Especially Walker. She'd never met anyone quite like him.

CHAPTER 19

Walker sat in the office at Jimmy's doing paperwork. But none of the numbers were adding up. Probably because his mind kept wandering. Thinking about Aspen. Their time together. The fact he was seeing her tonight. The unfortunate reality that she was leaving town tomorrow. All these thoughts bounced around his head, making it impossible to concentrate. He ran his fingers through his hair in exasperation.

He looked up as Tara walked into the office.

"Hey, I saw you're off tonight. Got any plans?" She lounged against the doorframe.

He looked down at the papers spread on the desk, wanting to dodge her question. "Ah... I'm going to happy hour at Blue Heron Cottages." He glanced up.

Tara raised her eyebrow. "Oh?"

"Yes." He frowned at her. "No big deal."

Tara rolled her eyes. "You should tell her, you know."

"Tell who what?" he asked innocently, knowing darn well who Tara was talking about.

"Aspen. Tell her."

"Tell her what?" He shuffled some papers on the desk, avoiding her hard, knowing stare.

"That you care about her." Tara stood with both hands on her hips, not to be deterred.

He laughed. "But I just met her. That's ridiculous." Only it wasn't ridiculous. He did have feelings for her, and his heart jolted in his chest just thinking about her leaving.

"Don't be such a dope. Tell her how you feel."

"She's leaving, sis. You know that."

"And they have roads between here and Georgia. They have planes now, too. Have you heard of those?"

"I don't think she wants so many complications in her life."

"You won't know until you talk to her, will you?" Tara shook her head. "You can be so dense sometimes. Tell her." She shook her head slowly, a look of exasperation on her face. She spun on her heels and stalked out of the office.

He pushed the chair away from the desk, staring out the window. Should he talk to Aspen tonight? It didn't make a lot of sense, though. She was leaving tomorrow. And they'd just met, he reminded himself. He couldn't really already have feelings for her. She was just fun and easy to talk to.

And fascinated him.

And made his pulse race every time she walked into Jimmy's.

He let out a long sigh. He was a goner. He had fallen for her. It didn't matter that it had only been a few days. He was going to miss her terribly when she left.

So, should he do something about it? Should he talk to her? Could they try to do something long-distance? But his life was crazy busy here at Jimmy's. It wasn't like he could keep taking days off to go up to Georgia to see her. And her new job probably would keep her busy, too.

It was probably best to just keep his thoughts to himself.

Probably.

He sprung up from his seat, abandoning his

poor attempt at completing some bookwork, and strode out of the office. He passed Tara in the main part of the restaurant. "I'm headed out."

As he walked away, Tara called after him. "Tell her."

His sister could be so exasperating.

Especially when she was right…

CHAPTER 20

Violet looked around the courtyard. Almost everything was ready for her happy hour. She really enjoyed these small gatherings on Fridays. She'd finally gotten some Adirondack chairs and set them in groupings in the courtyard, too. This winter she might put a fire pit out here for the chilly nights she was told they might have in January or February. Or at least what Florida called chilly. Besides, a fire pit would give a nice cheery ambiance.

She hoped that Melody and Ethan would show up tonight. She enjoyed getting to know both of them better. So far, they were her closest friends here in Moonbeam.

Rob walked up with a large tray in his arms. "Where do you want the appetizers?"

"Just set the tray on the table. Thanks for picking them up for me."

"No problem. Gave me a chance to see Evelyn."

"Is she coming?"

"No, she's working tonight. But I'm going to meet up with her after she closes the cafe."

She adjusted where Rob had placed the tray, then continued filling a galvanized washtub filled with ice, beer, and soda. She placed a couple of bottles of white wine deep down into the ice. A handful of red wine bottles were set on the table along with a tray of wine glasses and a stack of napkins with starfish and shells on them. A vase of fresh-cut flowers adorned one end of the table. Should be plenty. Guests had checked into two more cottages for the weekend, which pleased her.

She moved the tray again. Then the vase. Then stood back and stared at the table.

Rob laughed. "It looks fine. Quit messing with it."

"I want it to look perfect."

"It does."

She saw Melody and Ethan coming into the courtyard and waved to them. Great, her suggestion had worked. They had come here together. Maybe sometime they'd even have a real date. If Ethan ever worked up his nerve. Or if Melody ever noticed the way he looked at her.

She glanced across the courtyard to see Willow and Derek headed toward the table. "Okay, here we go. Another happy hour." She tilted her head toward the couple.

When Robbie turned to glance over toward Willow's cottage, she slyly moved the tray one more time. There, now that was perfect.

CHAPTER 21

Aspen opened the door to find Walker standing there. She sucked in a quick breath as her heart began pounding. He looked so incredibly handsome.

A warm, welcoming smile spread across his face. "Hey, you look great," he said.

She glanced down at yet another sundress Willow had given her, thankful to be out of her old, worn clothes. Not that it would matter after today. She'd be back in her old clothes and her old life. But she didn't want to think about that now.

She stepped outside. "You look pretty great yourself." She tried to sound nonchalant. Friendly. Though she wasn't certain she pulled it off.

He took her elbow and led her toward the crowd gathered in the courtyard. He grabbed a beer for both of them, and they walked over to where Willow and Derek were standing.

Walker nodded at them and raised his beer. "Cheers."

They all clinked their drinks. "Cheers."

She didn't know why she was so nervous. It was just a simple happy hour gathering. But nonetheless, she shifted nervously from foot to foot, her hand slightly shaking as she raised her beer to her lips.

She saw Rose in the distance and waved to her. Rose took a glass of wine from Violet and walked over to them.

"Rose, I'd like you to meet everyone. This is my sister, Willow, and her husband, Derek."

"Nice to meet both of you." Rose lifted her glass slightly in greeting.

"And this is Walker."

"Ah, Walker, so nice to meet you, too. Aspen has spoken highly of you and your family."

She blushed. She didn't want Walker to think she went around talking about him all the time.

"My family is quite taken with Aspen, too." He gave her an irresistible grin. Not that she had any resistance where he was concerned. "We're going to miss her working at Jimmy's. She's great. Really helped us out when we needed it."

The heat of the blush grew to almost the boiling point. These compliments needed to end.

"It was nothing." She played down her helping and changed the subject. "Rose used to come here to the cottages years ago.

"You did?" Willow asked. "What was it like then?"

"Well, it had gotten kind of run down over the years, but I loved it. I looked forward to coming each year. And the beach here is so lovely, isn't it?"

"It is. The water is such a beautiful shade of turquoise." Aspen glanced over at the water. She would miss it. She glanced at Walker, who was staring at her, a far-away expression on his face as if he was lost in thought.

"I talked to Violet, and I'm going to stay for a few more weeks," Rose said.

"Oh, that would be so nice. It's so wonderful here. Derek and I were talking about coming back here soon and bringing our son, Eli. He'd love the beach."

Willow hadn't said a word to her about coming back here to the cottages. But then, maybe she wanted a vacation with just her, Derek, and Eli. A family vacation.

But still, it hurt a little. She felt like Blue Heron Cottages were her and Willow's special place. Where they first came when they found out they were sisters.

But so much was changing now. Willow was making plans without her. She had to leave and find a new job. Start a new life.

Suddenly, a wave of loneliness settled over her. Which was kind of silly, considering she was standing here surrounded by people.

But come tomorrow, all this would be over. She'd be back on her own. And suddenly, that didn't sound very great to her. Her hard-won self-reliance that she'd always been proud of seemed kind of empty now.

As the happy hour wound down, Walker leaned close to Aspen. "Hey, do you want to go for a walk on the beach?" He needed some time alone with her. And then he'd figure out what he was going to say to her. If anything.

"Sure," she said as he took her empty beer bottle.

"Let me go put these in recycling. Be right back."

He could feel her gaze as he crossed to the recycling bin and walked back to her.

"Willow, we're going to take a walk. Do you and Derek want to come?" Aspen turned to her sister.

No, that's not what he meant.

Not what he wanted.

He wanted time *alone* with her.

Willow glanced over at him, a small smile on her lips. "No, I don't think so. I think we might just head to the porch and sit awhile."

Yes! Good for Willow and Derek. They didn't really need a long old beach walk now, did they?

"Ready?" He turned to Aspen, happy it would just be the two of them.

She nodded.

They headed toward the beach while he debated whether he should take her hand or not. The debate lasted all the way to the water's edge and still, he hadn't taken her hand.

Why not? Tara's words mocked him in his head.

They dropped their shoes on the sand and headed down the shoreline, the water lapping over their bare feet. His mind raced, trying to decide what to say. As they walked around the bend on the beach, he stopped. "Aspen? Could we talk?"

"Sure." She stopped beside him and looked at him with those incredible brown eyes of hers. The ones flecked with gold. The ones that lit up when she smiled. The ones that would haunt him after she left.

His thoughts bounced around and he struggled to find the right words. He reached down and took her hands in his. Her hands were cold and he could feel the warmth of his melt into hers.

About time. Somehow Tara was taunting him when she wasn't even here.

Ignoring his sister talking to him in his mind, he looked down at Aspen. Where to start? "I've really enjoyed the time we've spent together this week."

"So have I." She gave him a shy smile.

"I…" He laughed. "I'm afraid I'm having a hard time figuring out what to say to you."

Her brow creased between her eyes. "Why?"

He let out a long breath. "Because I have so

much I want to say. But I'm not sure if I should say it."

"Just say what you're thinking," she encouraged him.

Ha. As if. His thoughts were ricocheting all around. How could he wrangle them in and talk coherently?

So he did the next best thing.

He leaned down, placed a hand along her jawline, and tilted her face up. Her gaze locked with this. Then he settled his lips on hers. For the kiss he'd been craving for days. Her hand grasped his waist. He circled his arms around her, pulling her close.

He finally ended the kiss and pulled her close to him, wrapping her securely in his arms. They stood like that for a few minutes. Silent, as the world continued to swirl around them, but they were locked into the moment, just the two of them.

She finally stepped back and looked at him, questioning him with her eyes.

He grinned. "I've been wanting to do that all week."

"You have?" Her eyes grew wider.

"I have. I don't know what you've done to

me… but I can't get you out of my mind. I think you've bewitched me."

"And you, me," she said softly as she reached up and touched her lips.

"I don't suppose you could stay a while longer?" he asked, holding his breath. Just a bit more time so they could sort all this out.

Her eyes filled with sadness, darkening, turning a chestnut brown. "No, that's just not possible."

Hope dashed inside him, crumbling into tiny grains of sand running through an hourglass. He just hadn't had enough time with her.

CHAPTER 22

As much as she'd love to stay and have more time with Walker, she couldn't. She couldn't afford to live in Moonbeam. And she didn't want him to find out about her life before Moonbeam any more than she wanted Willow to find out. She'd leave and find a new job. A *good* one this time. And a nice place to live. Then no one would be the wiser to the pathetic lifestyle she had now.

But that kiss.

That kiss. It had taken away her breath, her thoughts. Everything had disappeared, and it was like it had only been the two of them. The only two in the whole world.

But that was part of the problem, wasn't it? She wasn't from his world. He had family and money and was going to run an entire restaurant soon. A stunning accomplishment at his age.

She wasn't right for him. She brought nothing to the relationship.

"The kiss was kind of mind-blowing though, wasn't it?" He gave her an impish grin, interrupting her thoughts.

She smiled reluctantly. "It was… nice."

"Wow, if it was only *nice*, I should try it again." He leaned in and kissed her again. She clung to his arms to keep her balance. To keep any connection to this world. She kissed him back, wanting it to go on forever. And yet regretting it because it would only make it that much harder to leave.

She sighed when he finally ended it.

"So? Better than just nice?" His mouth curved into a lopsided grin.

"Yes, better than just nice." She smiled back at him.

She was going to miss so much about him. The ease of talking to him. His teasing. His smiles.

And now she was going to miss his kisses.

"I wish I could stay. But I have to go. The job, you know." And that was partially right. She did need to go and find a job somewhere where she could actually afford to live. She'd looked at rentals here, and even one that looked horrid—and she'd lived in some crummy places—was five times what she'd paid for her last apartment. She hurried on. "This week has been wonderful. And complicated. *So* complicated. I'm ready for life to be a little less complicated. Simple. Predictable." She gave a little laugh.

He stepped back as a brief look of hurt flitted across his face.

"I mean… I found out about Willow, about my father. So many changes. I need time to sort everything out."

He nodded, but his face was masked now, showing little emotion. "I understand. And we should head back to the cottages. You probably need to pack."

No, she wanted to stay out here on the beach with him for hours. Talk. Laugh. Kiss. But what good would that do? It would just be that much harder to leave. "You're right. We should head back."

They walked back to the cottages in silence. Side by side, but so apart. She no longer felt the connection to him that she'd felt before. It was like a wall had dropped between them. A very tall wall that could not be climbed over. Her heart squeezed, and she tried to ignore it. This was for the best. They'd had a few fun days. That's all it was.

They walked into the courtyard at the cottages. Violet had cleared up all evidence of happy hour. The stars were starting to light up the sky above them, oblivious to the turmoil inside her. Twinkling above like it was just any other night. He walked her to her cottage porch, and she slowly climbed the stairs.

He stood at the bottom, looking up at her. "I'm going to miss you, Aspen Caldwell."

"And I'll miss you, Walker Bodine." She choked out the words.

"Good luck with this next stage of your life. I hope you find your father."

She nodded. "Thanks."

He gave her a long, lingering stare as if memorizing her. Imprinting her image. She understood. She felt the same way as she stared at him.

He suddenly bounded up the steps, took her hands, and kissed her. A long, lingering kiss that almost brought her to her knees.

He pulled away and gave her one last sad

smile. "Goodbye, Aspen. I won't forget my time with you."

"Goodbye, Walker."

He climbed down the steps and walked away, crossing the courtyard, never looking back. Her heart broke into a million pieces as he disappeared. She'd never felt this way about someone before. Which probably was a good thing, because the pain searing through her now was almost more than she could bear.

CHAPTER 23

Aspen got up early the next morning and finished the packing she hadn't been able to make herself do last night. She'd just sat by the window for hours, staring out at the courtyard where Walker had disappeared.

This had been the most tumultuous week of her life, and she was having a hard time finding her footing. She glanced out the window and saw it was just beginning to lighten.

Time for one last morning watching the sunrise. She set down the pretty sundress from Willow that she was folding, smoothing its fabric into nice, neat folds. She hurried outside embracing the warm morning air. Crossing the beach, she found Rose sitting beside the water.

She smiled at Rose through the sadness that had clung to her since Walker walked away from her last night. "My last morning." She plopped down beside her.

"Such a shame. I'll miss you." Rose's eyes shone with sincerity. "You've been a nice surprise friend."

"I'll miss you, too." She fought back her emotions. And to her dismay, a lone tear trailed down her cheek. She dashed it away.

Rose took her hand. "It's hard to leave here, isn't it?"

She stared at her hand in Rose's warm, weathered hand. "It's… it's more than that. It's everything. Everything is so messed up." Suddenly, all the emotions of the week caught up with her, overwhelmed her. To the point she could barely breathe. She swallowed trying to fight back her tears.

"What's messed up? Tell me." Rose squeezed her hand. "It will help to talk it out."

And suddenly the words wanted to pour out of her, and she couldn't hold them back. Didn't want to hold them back. She desperately needed to talk to someone, and Rose was the closest person she had to a friend right now.

"Well... you see... I... I haven't told Willow the truth about me. About my past. I don't even have a job to go to. Or a place to live." She looked at Rose and took a deep breath. "I'm living out of my car right now. Everything I own is in the trunk. How pathetic is that?"

"Oh, hon. I had no idea."

"I'll find something. I always do. I just couldn't bear to let Willow know what a failure I've been with my life." She closed her eyes against the tears she was trying so hard to control.

"I don't think you're a failure. I think you're strong. You're a giving, lovely woman."

"I don't want her to know. We're so different. She's successful and rich and... well, she has everything."

"She'd understand. You should tell her."

"I... can't." She squeezed her eyes shut at the thought.

"At some point, you need to believe in yourself. Really believe. It will turn your life around. Go after your dreams. Believe in them. I have every confidence you can do whatever you set your mind to."

She stared at Rose, who believed in her

more than she believed in herself. When had she quit trying for something more? Settled for her flighty life? Stopped trying for a better job, a better life? When had she settled for just existing?

"Anyway, I think you should at least consider telling her. Don't start this new relationship with your sister having secrets."

She wasn't sure. She just didn't want to see a look of disappointment, or worse yet, pity, in Willow's eyes.

Rose's eyes narrowed. "And is there something else going on?"

A tiny laugh escaped her lips. "How do you read me so well after such a short time?"

Rose shrugged and gave her a gentle smile.

"Yes, there is more." The heat of a blush crept across her cheeks. "Walker kissed me last night."

"And how do you feel about that?"

"I feel like I found this wonderful man at the wrong time in my life."

"You care about him, don't you?"

"I do. I really like him. But it's just not meant to be. Different worlds. Wrong timing."

"And you didn't tell him how you felt after he kissed you?"

"I couldn't." She'd been too afraid. Afraid that he didn't feel the same way. Though... his eyes said he cared. But he probably felt like her. That their timing was off.

"I think you should go find Walker and tell him how you feel. You shouldn't let a chance at love disappear just because of fear. Of not having all the answers. True love is worth all the sacrifices you might have to make."

There was a story there in Rose's eyes, she could tell. Like maybe she was talking from experience.

"So go talk to him." Rose's eyes filled with encouragement and support.

"I don't think I can. We said our goodbyes. It's probably best to leave it as it is. We had a wonderful week. That's all."

"And is your heart saying that is enough?"

She reached up and placed her hand over her traitorous heart. Was it enough? It would have to be because it would be too complicated any other way.

And what if he didn't feel the same way? There was every chance it was just some fling for him. For all she knew, he probably had them all the time with visitors to town. Or maybe he did feel something for her, but would he still feel that way if he knew the truth about her? Would he leave her then?

"You should talk to both Willow and Walker and tell them the truth. Telling the truth is very freeing. Cathartic. And you might be surprised what happens when you open up to people you care about and tell them the truth. Let them in."

Maybe Rose was right. But she wasn't sure she was brave enough to take Rose's suggestion. What if she saw disappointment, or worse yet, pity in their eyes if they knew the truth about her?

What if Walker didn't feel the same way about her that she did about him?

But what... what if Rose was right, and she took a chance and things *did* work out?

She wavered on the tightrope of indecision, unsure which path she wanted to take. The safe path of leaving with no one knowing the truth? Or taking a risk? Telling them both about her past, telling Walker how she felt.

She turned to Rose, her heart skipping beats at the choice before her. "I'm just not sure I can do it. That I can tell them."

Rose stood. "I'm sure you'll make the decision that's right for you. But remember, you are stronger than you're giving yourself credit for. Believe in yourself."

Rose headed back to the cottages in slow, measured steps, but Aspen stayed on the beach. She fingered a shell, watching the waves roll to shore and weighing Rose's advice.

CHAPTER 24

Aspen peeked out the window. The courtyard was empty. No sign of Willow. Good, then she could load her things into her car without anyone seeing her. She needed to put some of it in the trunk and sure didn't want anyone to see all that she had crammed in there. Her entire life's possessions fit in that trunk as embarrassing as that was. In spite of Rose's advice, she just couldn't make herself go knock on Willow's door and say, "Oh, hey, I'm jobless and homeless. Look what a great catch you got in a sister."

She headed out to the car with a box of odds and ends. Mostly things left over from the gift basket Magnolia's lawyer had sent. She'd saved most of it. It would help tide her over until she found a job. She carried the box to the back of her car, popped the trunk, and frowned. She'd have to rearrange things for the box to fit. She set it on the ground and started to move the items in her trunk around.

"Aspen? What's all this?" Willow stood beside her, looking into the trunk full of stacks of clothes, a few pots and pans, a box of food, sheets and blankets, and a pillow in a unicorn pillowcase she'd picked up at a thrift shop for a quarter.

Her pulse quickened. "Um… it's just stuff."

"Why is all this in your trunk?"

"I… uh…" Think fast, woman. Come up with a plausible excuse. "Oh… it's… uh."

"Didn't your movers get everything packed up?" Willow frowned.

Ah, she was saved. "Just things I wanted to bring with me." Willow didn't have to know it was everything she owned. So she wasn't really lying to her.

"Oh." Willow looked at the stuffed trunk again, then turned to her. "You didn't give me your new address."

"Oh, I have it somewhere. I can't quite put

my finger on it." That was almost the truth, too. She'd be able to put her finger on it when she, you know, actually found a place.

"Anyway, I was talking to Derek. How about you come up to Jacksonville? You could follow us up there. Come meet Eli. Spend the night. Then, I was thinking I could ride up with you to Georgia. I could help you move in. We could spend some more time together. Then I'd fly back home."

Now that wouldn't work, would it? There was no place to move into. Her heart pounded as she looked for an escape. "Oh, you don't need to do that. I've got it all under control. Besides, you'd miss Eli. You've been gone a week now."

She laughed softly. "Oh, he's enjoying being spoiled by his grandmother. I do miss him. But we'll spend tonight with him. Maybe we could stay Sunday, too? Then head up on Monday?"

"I don't want you to do that."

"You don't?" Willow frowned.

"I mean, you have your family, your job. I can't take you away from that."

"But I'd love to help. We'll get you unpacked. I'll see your new place. I'm really good at decorating. We could spruce the place up a bit. Make it feel like home in no time. It would be fun."

Aspen stood there staring at her sister, who looked so eager to help. But she couldn't accept that help. Because she had no place to move into.

Rose and Violet came walking up to them, so she was saved from answering for a moment.

"Are you packing up? I'm sorry to see you leave," Violet said.

Rose looked into the trunk of the car, then looked closely at her but didn't say anything more.

"I sure loved having you two here. Come back any time." Violet's smile was so... welcoming.

She was going to miss this. Miss Moonbeam. Miss her morning talks with Rose. Miss the Bodines...

Suddenly, a lone tear ran down her cheek. Followed by another. But that wasn't possible, because she didn't cry. Never. Well, except for this morning on the beach with Rose. What was wrong with her this week?

"Oh, Aspen. What's wrong?" Willow hugged her.

"Nothing," she lied as she clung to her sister and more tears fell.

Willow stepped back and looked at her. "Yes, something is wrong. I know it. You have to tell me."

Rose looked at her encouragingly and nodded her support.

She took a deep breath and swiped away the tears. "I… I don't have a place to go to in Georgia."

Willow's brow creased. "You haven't found an apartment yet?"

She let out a long sigh. "It's more than that. I haven't found a job yet. I don't really know where I'm heading for sure. I lost my last job just before I came here. I…" She turned and waved an arm at the overflowing trunk of her car. "I let my apartment go and these are all my things. Everything I own. As you can see, it's not much." Her face flushed with embarrassment.

Willow looked stunned for a moment but recovered quickly. "Why didn't you tell me all this? Is this why you haven't talked much about your past?"

She nodded.

"You didn't need to keep this a secret."

"But you're so successful and you have a

nice house, a nice family. Everything. I didn't want you to think I'm some kind of loser."

"You're not a loser," Willow said. "You're an incredibly strong woman. You've survived a lot. I admire you. I don't think I could have been that strong."

"You admire me?"

"Of course. Look what you've overcome. And you haven't become bitter. You just keep overcoming the curves that life throws you."

Rose smiled at her, her eyes twinkling as if saying, "see?"

"Oh, you should come live with us until you find a new job." Willow's eyes brightened.

"No, I'm not going to take charity from you. I just… can't."

"But you're my sister. It's just helping you out. You'd do it for me, wouldn't you?"

"I can't. I need to do this on my own."

"Would a job help?" Violet stepped forward. "Here at the cottages. I can offer you part-time."

"Oh, Violet, that's so nice. But I can't afford to live here in Moonbeam. I looked at apartments. They are so out of my budget. And this old car isn't reliable enough to find a place more inland and affordable."

Violet smiled. "And I have a solution for that, too. There's an old cottage behind the owner's cottage. I haven't fixed it up yet. Well, I fixed the roof so it wouldn't leak. It only has a window unit air conditioner now. But if you'd agree to paint it and fix it up some, you could live there rent-free."

"I couldn't—"

"You could," Violet insisted. "You'd be doing me a favor, rehabbing it for me. And if you come to work for me part-time, Robbie will quit bugging me to get help."

"And I bet that Walker would hire you on at Jimmy's, too," Violet said. "He couldn't stop raving about what a great job you did there and how sorry he was that you were leaving."

"I don't know…"

Rose placed her hand on her arm. "You know, sometimes it's okay to take some help. You don't have to do everything alone."

Willow nodded her head briskly. "I think this is a wonderful solution. You love it here in Moonbeam. You said so last night. You'd have a place to stay, a job. And I could come visit you!"

She looked at each one of them, still uncertain. But maybe Rose was right. It was okay to take this help.

"Really, it would help me out if you stay." Violet's eyes shone with enthusiasm.

"I…" Her mouth broke into a grin. "Okay. I'll stay."

Willow clapped her hands. "This is perfect."

It did sound kind of perfect. She'd never felt more at home than she had here in Moonbeam with the friends she'd made.

"Go find Walker. Tell him." Willow laughed. "He'll be very pleased."

"Yes, I think you have quite a few things to say to Walker." Rose flashed a knowing smile.

She slammed the trunk of her car. "I think I will."

"Derek and I will be here for another hour or so. We'll wait for you to get back here."

"Okay, I won't be long." She turned to Violet. "Thank you."

"No, thank you. I'll finally be getting the help I need. And I'm sure we can coordinate your schedule with Jimmy's."

"If they give me a job."

Violet laughed. "Oh, they will."

She turned and, with one last wave of her hand, briskly walked down the drive to the sidewalk and hurried to Jimmy's. Her heart pounded furiously in her chest. So many changes so quickly. But it felt right to stay here in Moonbeam. It did. She just hoped Walker was pleased, too.

CHAPTER 25

Walker turned around at the sound of Tara's voice. "Walker, there's someone here to see you." His sister stood there positively grinning at him.

"Who?"

"I sent them out to wait for you on the wharf. Over at the side."

"You didn't answer who it is." He rolled his eyes. "I'm kinda busy."

"Not too busy for this," Tara insisted.

He let out a long sigh, set down the tray he held, and shook his head, mumbling about his impossible sister as he headed out of the restaurant and out to the wharf, heading over to where it wrapped around the side of the building.

He stopped short when he got there.

No, it couldn't be. She was gone. They'd said their goodbyes last night. A fact his heart had been painfully aware of all day. He swallowed. Why had she come? He didn't think he could take another goodbye.

"Aspen?"

She turned from the railing, a wide smile on her face. "There you are. Tara said she'd find you."

"She did. What are you doing here?"

"It seems like I'm in need of a part-time job."

He frowned. "What? I don't understand." His thoughts bounced around, trying to figure out what she was saying to him.

"If I can find this part-time job, then I'm going to stay in Moonbeam."

The air rushed out of his lungs. "You're what?"

"Violet gave me a place to stay rent-free if I fix up the cottage in return. And she offered me a part-time job at Blue Heron Cottages. But... I'd need more than part-time work..." She looked at him expectantly.

"But your job in Georgia?"

"About that. It's a long story and I'll tell you

later. But for now, just know I want to stay here."

He let out a whoop, strode the few steps to her, and picked her up, swinging her around in a circle. "You've got a job here. Of course. We'd love to have you." He set her down and stood there grinning like a fool. And he didn't care. He could look foolish. He was so extraordinarily happy right now.

"That's what Tara said, but I wanted to be sure it was okay with you."

"Okay with me? It's fabulous. Great. Wonderful."

She smiled up at him. "I'm glad that worked out, then."

He took her hands in his, staring down at them for a long moment, thinking they felt so right there in his. "I'm so glad that you're staying here in Moonbeam. I had so much I wanted to say to you last night. Tell you how I felt. But... you were so set on leaving. You didn't want complications. I swear it broke my heart to walk away and leave you last night."

"Mine, too." She looked up into his eyes. "So, your goodbye kiss was really nice. But you think you could swing a welcome back kiss?"

He grinned at her. "I think I could manage

that." And he leaned down and settled his lips on hers, wrapping her in his arms, tight against him. "Best news ever," he whispered in her ear as he held her close.

~

Aspen and Walker headed back to the cottages, and she told him her whole story. How she'd lost her job and her home. That everything she owned was in her car.

"You could have told me before this. At the beginning when we first started talking," Walker said. "You don't have to hide anything from me."

"I was afraid of what people would think when they found out."

"Don't you know that I admire your strength? What you've gone through? It hasn't broken you. You came out strong and spirited."

Her heart pounded and happiness rushed through her. It had all worked out to tell the truth. To go after what she wanted. She was staying in Moonbeam. Everything was falling into place.

When they got back to the cottages, she said

her goodbyes to Willow and Derek, who promised to come visit soon and bring Eli.

Willow held her tight in a hug. "I'll miss you."

"I'll miss you, too." She hugged her sister back.

"Call me. Call me lots," Willow insisted.

"I will. And you call any time. I can't wait to meet Eli."

She and Walker stood in the drive as Derek and Willow drove away. She should be sad that her sister was leaving, but instead, she was content. Because Willow was coming back soon. Just like a regular family visit like regular families did.

"Come on, let me help you move your things into your new place." They walked over to her car and grabbed some boxes.

They climbed the stairs to the porch, and she opened the door, stepping inside. That same strange feeling she'd felt when she first saw Willow crept through her. She frowned, looking around the cottage. It felt so familiar.

She turned to Walker as he set down a box. "I have the strangest feeling like I've been here before."

"Like deja vu?

"Yes… but I can't have been here, can I?" The strange tingling feeling rose to a crescendo. She gasped. "Wait…" She ran to the back bedroom. A tiny room with sun beams filtering through the lone window and dancing on the worn wooden floor. Walker followed close behind her.

She tugged open the closet door and looked carefully. She threw her arm up triumphantly. "Look. I *have* been here."

"What?"

"I remember that." She pointed to initials carved into the far back corner of the closet. A.C. in jagged letters.

Walker peered inside the closet. "A.C. Aspen Caldwell."

"Yes, I remember doing that. I think Magnolia and I lived here."

"Really?"

"Yes, must have. But why were we here?"

"Maybe just one of the places she moved you to? Didn't you say you moved around a lot?"

"We did. But I think… well, I feel like we stayed here longer than we usually stayed places." She shrugged. "I guess I'll never know, though, will I?"

"But you know you were here." Walker took her hand and led her out to the main room.

"It's funny that life would bring me right back here, isn't it?"

"I'm glad it did." He took her into his arms and kissed her. Suddenly she felt like she belonged. Right here in his arms. Right here at Blue Heron Cottages. Right here in *this* cottage. The pieces of her life just fell into place.

He pulled back and searched her face. "So, you're happy?"

"I've never been more happy or more content in my life."

"Then you're right where you belong." He kissed her again.

And she did feel like she belonged. Finally. For the first time in her life.

CHAPTER 26

R ose sat alone on the porch of her cottage watching the sunset explode across the sky. Emmett used to love watching the sunsets with her from this very spot. The day had passed quietly. No fanfare. No celebration. No gifts. No Emmett.

No one in the whole world knew how special today was.

Her fiftieth anniversary. Alone. At the very spot she'd spent almost every anniversary. Only this time without her beloved husband.

She raised her glass to the dying light of the day. "Good night, my love. I miss you so very much."

The breeze swept across her cheek and she

swore, for just a tiny moment, she was *certain* it was Emmett's touch. She reached up and touched her cheek. "Ah, Emmett. Life just isn't the same," she whispered up to the night sky above.

But being back here at the cottages helped. She felt him here. The memories were strong here. Staying for a few more weeks was a good decision.

"Thanks for insisting I come back here again. You were right. It's been good for me. I'm going to stay for a bit."

Dear Reader,

I hope you enjoyed the beginning of the Blue Heron Cottages series. What's up next? Book two, Walks along the Shore. A couple arrives at the cottages for their wedding, but there is trouble between the maid of honor and the best man. Oh, and more problems. Like with the wedding planner *and* the wedding dress. Violet, Rose, and Aspen along with the other Moonbeam characters will, of course, be part of the story. Don't miss it.

Thanks for reading my stories. I truly appreciate each and every one of my readers.

Happy reading,

Kay

ALSO BY KAY CORRELL

COMFORT CROSSING ~ THE SERIES

The Shop on Main - Book One

The Memory Box - Book Two

The Christmas Cottage - A Holiday Novella
(Book 2.5)

The Letter - Book Three

The Christmas Scarf - A Holiday Novella (Book 3.5)

The Magnolia Cafe - Book Four

The Unexpected Wedding - Book Five

The Wedding in the Grove (crossover short story
between series - Josephine and Paul from The
Letter.)

LIGHTHOUSE POINT ~ THE SERIES

Wish Upon a Shell - Book One

Wedding on the Beach - Book Two

Love at the Lighthouse - Book Three

Cottage near the Point - Book Four

Return to the Island - Book Five

Bungalow by the Bay - Book Six

CHARMING INN ~ Return to Lighthouse Point

One Simple Wish - Book One

Two of a Kind - Book Two

Three Little Things - Book Three

Four Short Weeks - Book Four

Five Years or So - Book Five

Six Hours Away - Book Six

Charming Christmas - Book Seven

SWEET RIVER ~ THE SERIES

A Dream to Believe in - Book One

A Memory to Cherish - Book Two

A Song to Remember - Book Three

A Time to Forgive - Book Four

A Summer of Secrets - Book Five

A Moment in the Moonlight - Book Six

MOONBEAM BAY ~ THE SERIES

The Parker Women - Book One

The Parker Cafe - Book Two

A Heather Parker Original - Book Three

The Parker Family Secret - Book Four

Grace Parker's Peach Pie - Book Five

The Perks of Being a Parker - Book Six

BLUE HERON COTTAGES ~ THE SERIES

A six-book series coming in 2022.

Memories of the Beach - Book One

Walks along the Shore - Book Two

WIND CHIME BEACH ~ A stand-alone novel

INDIGO BAY ~ Save by getting Kay's complete collection of stories previously published separately in the multi-author Indigo Bay series. The three stories are all interconnected.

Sweet Days by the Bay - the collection

ABOUT THE AUTHOR

Kay writes sweet, heartwarming stories that are a cross between women's fiction and contemporary romance. She is known for her charming small towns, quirky townsfolk, and enduring strong friendships between the women in her books.

Kay lives in the Midwest of the U.S. and can often be found out and about with her camera, taking a myriad of photographs which she likes to incorporate into her book covers. When not lost in her writing or photography, she can be found spending time with her ever-supportive husband, knitting, or playing with her puppies —two cavaliers and one naughty but adorable Australian shepherd. Kay and her husband also love to travel. When it comes to vacation time, she is torn between a nice trip to the beach or the mountains—but the mountains only get considered in the summer—she swears she's allergic to snow.

Learn more about Kay and her books at
kaycorrell.com

While you're there, sign up for her newsletter to
hear about new releases, sales, and giveaways.

WHERE TO FIND ME:
kaycorrell.com
authorcontact@kaycorrell.com

Join my Facebook Reader Group. We have lots
of fun and you'll hear about sales and new
releases first!
www.facebook.com/groups/KayCorrell/

I love to hear from my readers. Feel free to
contact me at authorcontact@kaycorrell.com

f facebook.com/KayCorrellAuthor

⊙ instagram.com/kaycorrell

℗ pinterest.com/kaycorrellauthor

ⓐ amazon.com/author/kaycorrell

BB bookbub.com/authors/kay-correll

Made in the USA
Las Vegas, NV
17 May 2023

72176568R10163